THE
OVAL
AMULET

THE OVAL AMULET

by

Lucy Cullyford Babbitt

1 8 17
HARPER & ROW, PUBLISHERS

Cambridge, Philadelphia, San Francisco, London, Mexico City, São Paulo, Singapore, Sidney

NEW YORK

Library of Congress Cataloging in Publication Data
Babbitt, Lucy Cullyford.
    The oval amulet.

    Summary: Rebellious Paragrin discovers the signifi-
cance of an iron oval amulet she possesses and uses it
to restore the world to a better and older way of life
in which women and men live and rule as equals.
    [1. Fantasy.   2. Sex role—Fiction] I. Title.
PZ7.B113450v 1985   [Fic]   83–49479
ISBN 0–06–020299–8
ISBN 0–06–020301–3 (lib. bdg.)

THE OVAL AMULET

is dedicated to all those people
who, for better or for worse,
have helped to inspire the characters in this book.

And to my mother,
who, time and again,
has helped to inspire me.

Oh, Essai!
I know You are displeased by what
You see, but I have lived among them
now for forty years and have found that
these mortals act not in defiance,
but in passionate ignorance.
They believe what they do is right
and will not heed my warnings.

Still, two generations have passed
from power since the Unity was broken,
and although this body has grown old
watching the Amulets go from hand to hand,
each in its separate land, I have not
despaired of their reunion.

How can I explain the faith that I have
learned to keep in these people, blind
as they have been? Hold Your judgment a
little longer, Essai, I beg You.

For a change is coming to the Melde.
I can sense it.
At last.

—Jentessa

PART ONE

PART ONE

1

When Essai first sent the Half-Divines out upon the new world to found a colony, It didn't foresee that the beautiful river valley they had chosen for the site would become a place of sorrow and oppression. How could It have? People, with their quarrelsome dispositions, had not yet been created. Nevertheless it didn't take long, once the Half-Divines left the city to the care of their children the mortals, for It to see that the Melde would become a less-than-perfect extension of Its master plan. But no matter. Essai was interested in the odd ways of the earth and bemused by the pride of the people as they strode and stumbled through the centuries; perhaps It just didn't choose to see that with each passing rulership a little more of the old wisdom was forgotten. Good was done in spite of this forgetfulness, it's true, but very much bad was done because of it, and never was the Melde Colony in such a state of wretched disrepair as in the time after Zessiper and Ram, when a determined man named Trag ruled alone.

The Maker wasn't the only one to finally lose patience; Trag's righteous son, Strap, broke off, with his own little band of disciples, to find a home free from the violence and shameful living of the city. He found it, too—far up the River where the forest thins and the Green Mountains give way to hillsides. He claimed the place for his own at once, declared it a new Land of Decency—Lexterre—and together with the men of his clan, he cleared the ground and built a village before the first snow of winter even fell. Strap was barely a man when he left the Melde, but he knew even then what he wanted.

The years passed, and when the town took in its tenth bountiful harvest Strap proclaimed a holiday, a time to give thanks to the Maker and to honor the fertility of the earth with a Maiden Dance. Strap was especially fond of the Dance, for he had created it himself as a way to help initiate the girls into their proper women-lives, as helpmates to men. It was a grand celebration, and he was looking forward to it; but there was one, at least, who did not share in his enthusiasm.

"Paragrin! Oh, my Maker, will you look at yourself!"

The girl jumped at the suddenness of the shriek and nearly dropped a slain rabbit she had brought to the hallway.

"Put that away before it drips its blood on the floor," said Aridda. "Sweet Father, it's already on your skirt."

Paragrin looked across at her brother's mate with a tolerant stare, and put the rabbit outside. "It's a fat one," she said, easing the bow and quiver from her shoulder. "You can use it in a stew tonight, if you like."

Aridda stood her ground. "Where have you been?"

"Where do you think I've been?" Paragrin returned, and moved to go past her, but the woman put out her hand and blocked the way.

"Don't you know what time it is?"

"Of course. I heard the drum."

"And look at your clothes. One of the few chances you get to show the boys what you have to offer, and you smell like a bear."

Paragrin narrowed her eyes. "The boys don't smell any better. I know; I was following them out of the woods."

"I don't want to hear it," said Aridda. "Now go wash your hands and face, and put on a clean apron before you come outside. And *please*, Paragrin," she said, reaching for her hair, "you must keep all this beneath the cap. No one respects a girl with loose strands."

"It won't stay," said Paragrin, knocking aside the hand, and stuffing the hair beneath the fabric herself. "It's too long. Maybe if I cut—"

"Don't touch it!" the woman cried. "Now go. We're both of us late as it is." And she turned and hurried out the door.

Paragrin, her hands still working at her cap, walked slowly into the main room and bent over the water bucket that sat by the hearth. She was just about to rinse her face when she caught sight of her reflection

5

and stopped. She stared at it, then struck the water with her hand, dissolving the image.

Now Strap was a man who approved of perfection. He demanded it of himself, of his willing mate, Aridda, and of the entire cast of men, women, and children that populated his village. Needless to say, he was often disappointed. But on that fall day as he stood on the leader's stage, the calling-sticks for the drum still held in his hands, he felt life was almost perfect. There were the girls of the Joining age—so pretty with their white caps and pale skin—forming a circle in the center of the square; and there were the brown young men, still glistening from their hunt in the woods, forming another circle around them. How fine it was!

"Welcome, everyone, to the Maiden Dance!" he exclaimed.

Paragrin, standing—at last—with the others, ignored his enthusiasm and raised her eyes as slyly as possible to the outer circle. Where was he? There! Two boys to her left. She brightened. Kerk was the best looking in the village by far, and now he would be the last that she danced in front of, the one she'd be facing when the singing stopped. Strap called out sharply to end a friendly game of wrestling that Kerk had begun, and Paragrin smiled. Strap's disapproval endeared Kerk to her even more.

"And so," said Strap, regaining his composure, "if our young girls are ready, let the Dance of the Maiden Harvest commence!"

The children clapped in rhythm, and as the Joined

women began to sing, Paragrin forced another stray lock beneath her cap and confronted the first boy.

"It's bringing-in-the-harvest time," the musicians proclaimed,

"And ev'ry maiden in her prime
    Does dance before
    Each bachelor,
Her ripeness for to show,
Oh! her ripeness for to show."

"Skip, spin, bow your head," Paragrin mumbled as faces passed unnoticed before her; she was only interested in one. Second verse.

"For like the bounty in the fields,
    The maiden, too, her fruit she yields;
    And by a mate
    Will cultivate,
And make his garden grow,
Oh! and make his garden grow."

This verse ended with Ellagette landing opposite Kerk. Paragrin frowned. She disliked Ellagette; not only because she was beautiful, but because she and Kerk had been seen together. Often. She turned to look at them, and her eyes widened. Ellagette was doing some movement she had never seen before. Kerk seemed to like it. A lot. Boldly, he reached forward and held her by her swaying hips.

"What do you think you're doing, boy?" Nob cried. Nob was Paragrin's present partner, and another of Ellagette's "prospects." He was big, but not nearly as handsome as Kerk, Paragrin had decided. So, obviously, had Ellagette.

"Nothing yet," Kerk answered, and Nob knocked him to the ground. Kerk landed hard, but only grinned in retaliation—until he seized Nob by the ankles and tripped him.

"Make them stop!" yelled Paragrin, turning to Ellagette.

"Why?" returned the girl, watching with pleasure as the two grappled before her.

"What's happening?" Strap demanded, breaking through the crowd.

And then, to her horror, Paragrin saw Nob pulling his hunting blade from its sheath. Without a second thought, she threw herself against him and sent the both of them sprawling on the grass.

"Great Father Divine!" cried Strap. "Paragrin! What are you doing?"

She scrambled up, triumphant. "He was going to use his knife!" she said. "I saw it, and stopped him before—"

"That's a lie!" Nob said, rising to his feet. "Look, I haven't touched my blade."

Strap did look, and indeed, Nob's knife had slid innocently back in its sheath. Slowly, he moved his gaze to Paragrin. "Go home," he said, and picking up the cap that had fallen from her head, added, "and take this with you."

"But he—" Paragrin began.

"GO," Strap repeated. "Now."

Her eyes flashed, but she snatched the cap back again

and pushed through the staring crowd, her wild black hair, scandalous in its freedom, flying out behind her.

"Now what started all of this?" Strap demanded, and as he turned to speak to Nob, Kerk winked at Ellagette.

2

"This is going to stop," said Strap.

"I didn't do anything wrong!" Paragrin protested. "Nob lied. He *was* going to use his blade."

"It doesn't matter. It wasn't your affair! If you were really worried, why didn't you come tell me, or tell another man?"

"There wasn't time. He would have used it on Kerk."

"Paragrin!" Strap cried. "It was not your responsibility, don't you realize that? Girls do not leap upon men; I don't care if Nob had had a *spear*. I won't have it, I tell you, I won't. Ah, don't you see what I've tried to do here?" he continued wearily. "Why I cared enough to take my sister from the Melde?"

"Your *half* sister," Paragrin put in.

"Why that should make a difference to you, I'll never

understand," he returned. "The important thing is that I took you away from our father, and the tyranny he inflicts on his people. You were only seven when we left the Colony. Perhaps you don't remember."

"I remember well enough."

"Then you should see why we're so lucky to live *here.* Life is as it should be, in Lexterre! Women don't have to be rough anymore; they have freedom. Think of what lies ahead of you: a Joining, then children, a house of your own to keep!"

Paragrin made a face.

"And yet you've never learned to settle down and behave as a girl should. This afternoon was unforgivable. Brawling—in the middle of the Maiden Dance, no less!"

"I didn't start the brawl."

"Listen, Paragrin," said Strap, "I know you don't particularly care what I think, so I won't ask you to change your ways for me. Do it for the Divine Father! His will must prevail. Can't you see how your behavior must hurt Him?"

"I don't care!" said Paragrin. "I don't even believe in Him."

Strap paled. "You what?"

"I said I don't believe in Him! Not if He expects me to bend under your rule without a word, like Aridda does. A Maker could never be that hateful." She had had her say, and waited for Strap to reply, but he only stared at her, speechless. "Maybe I've said too much," she thought, and a knot of regret welled within her. Yet after a silence had passed, the horror in Strap's face seemed to clear, as if a burden had suddenly been lifted.

11

"It's all right, after all," she said to herself.

But it was not.

"Paragrin," said Strap, "you're going to leave."

"Leave this house?"

"Leave Lexterre."

"And go where?" she asked, astonished.

"Back to the other people of your kind. Back to the Melde."

"The Melde? But you—"

"I'm sorry," he said, "but I've done all I possibly could. I kept thinking that there was some way to reach you, to bring you back into the Maker's world. But now that you've denounced Him, well . . . I see now how wrong I was. I can't have you in the village, Paragrin. Tomorrow a man will take you downriver to the Colony."

"Strap! How can you—"

"There's nothing else I can do," he said. "It's a great embarrassment to me, yet in the end I think we'll both be happier." He started for the door, then paused. "To save me from any further disgrace," he added, "you might at least keep your hair from hanging in your face when you leave. It's disgusting." And with that, he turned and shut the door behind him.

"Rot you!" Paragrin cried. "I'm *glad* to leave!" The stiff fabric of the cap bent in her fist. "And I'll see you get more disgrace than you bargained for." She spun around, eyes wide, and seized the hunting blade that lay on her bed. Taking big knots of hair in hand, she dragged the knife across them again and again, until the thick locks were severed and fell in clumps to the

12

ground. She breathed hard as she stared at the tangles and wondered then why she didn't feel triumphant. With a gasp, she dropped the knife and sank to the floor among the curls, weeping.

She lay there for a long time, lamenting her fate, but finally, when she could cry no longer, she pulled herself up and tried to think of a brighter side to her banishment. Maybe the Melde wouldn't be as black as her brother had painted it. After all, it was he who had rebelled against their father, not she. She barely knew Trag. The only thing she really remembered was that he had thick black hair, like hers; and that he was large— abnormally large—and strong.

"Well, I don't have to run into him," she thought, as the image shimmered new and ominously in her mind. "I can always stay at the edges of the court, and—" She stopped, breathless. The edge of the court! Turning about, she reached under her bed and brought out a small wooden box, worn at the edges with age and handling. Carefully she lifted out its ancient contents: an old iron Oval, hung from a fine-linked chain. She held it gently in her palm, and remembered that day ten years ago, right before she had left the city.

There was the woman again in her mind, the sad but beautiful stranger who was kept prisoner in a tiny stone house at the edge of the central court. Who exactly she was, or why she was confined, Paragrin never knew, but the woman had a kind face, and often watched her from the little window in her cell.

One morning the guard who was usually posted by the house had disappeared, and suddenly through this window, the woman called out her name and beckoned to her. Paragrin remembered being alarmed at first, but when she looked back into those imploring eyes, she was filled with a terrible sense of longing and went to her. One small child stood before the faded beauty of the prisoner, and the woman had gazed down at her for several moments before stretching her arm through the window and dropping a bundle into her hands. She had urged then, in an impassioned whisper that Paragrin would never forget, "Keep this treasure well, my Own, my daughter, and until the great time comes, never, never show it to anyone!" That was all she had time to say. The guard returned and chased Paragrin away, and though she was puzzled by the gift of an oval-shaped iron, so cold and caked with dirt that it looked as if it had been buried, she never spoke to the woman again. The next day, Strap had taken her with him to find Lexterre.

"Well, I'll come back to you now, anyway," Paragrin promised, pressing the iron to her heart, "and in all these years . . . my mother . . . I still haven't shown it to anyone."

She rose then, fingering the Oval, and went over to the polished metal plate that hung on the wall. Slipping the chain around her neck, she lifted her eyes to meet the reflection—and gasped. A sickness rose in her as she saw the ruined shape of her hair, jagged and uneven, with a lock so short in front that it hung just above her eyes. "Oh, no," she moaned, gathering what was left of her tresses behind her head, "I look like a b—" The word faltered on her lips. She stared back at the image.

14

A minute later she was wielding the knife again, this time more carefully, an inch here, half an inch there, a long lock cut back above her shoulders. Finally, when her feet were buried in a mass of curls, she stepped back and laughed.

"I *am* a boy!" she exclaimed, and reached up to feel her new hair. How marvelously light it felt!

The next moment, she was at the door listening for voices. Another moment, and she was back again, holding in her arms the spoils from her brother's room: a bulky jacket, a pair of black pants, and big furry hunting boots, the ones that Aridda had made especially for him, out of bearskin.

Her blouse and narrow skirt were quickly discarded, and taking the pants in hand, she drew them on, delighting in the new sensation of cloth around her legs. The jacket followed, but was less successful, for with all its looseness, it still showed the bumps of her breasts beneath it. Paragrin considered this problem for a minute, then turned and cut a slice out of her blanket and, lifting her jacket up, wrapped it tightly around her chest. Her feminine curves flattened and disappeared beneath the cloth. It was wonderful. And finally, kicking off her slippers, she stuffed the toes of the boots with more bits of blanket and lowered her feet into their warmth.

She danced across the floor, reveling in the feel of the clothes and the great freedom of movement they gave her. Looking into the metal once more, she grinned. A tousle-haired boy, complete with costume, grinned back.

"So much for having to behave like a girl," she said. "All right, Strap, I'll go to the Melde. But I won't wait

15

for your escort. I'll go by myself. Tonight." She was just about to turn from the image, when her eye caught the glimmer of the Oval's chain through the long, open collar of the jacket. She paused, remembering her mother's words, then pulled the laces of the collar tight, so that the iron beneath was hidden.

Then she took up her bow and quiver of arrows, anchoring them both securely across her shoulders. Her blade she stuck firmly into the folds of a wide belt she had tied around her hips. At last she was ready.

Creeping back into the hall, she turned from the front entrance and stole along the passage to the back door.

The moon, full-grown and bright, hung low in the sky and glowed invitingly through the treetops. Taking a deep breath of autumn air, Paragrin felt the excitement rise within her. She walked quickly down the path that led to the River, then broke into a run, running with her legs finally free to stretch, away from the Land of Decency and along the wide grassy riverbank toward the Melde.

3

"Ho, there!"

Eyes wide and fingers clutching at the grass, Paragrin started from her sleep. The sun was high above her now, and as it shone down upon the trees and River, she remembered her flight the evening before. Yet landscape wasn't all she saw: standing over her were two of the boys from Lexterre—and one of them was Kerk.

He stared back at her, his brown arms crossed casually in front of him. "Hello again," he said. "And what are you?"

Paragrin's heart pounded. She got slowly to her feet, her gaze never leaving his face. "I . . . I . . ." she began.

"You . . . you . . . *what?*"

"I'm a boy!" she exclaimed.

"Good for you," he returned, and looked sideways

17

at his friend. "I meant, what's your *name*."

She looked back at him still, not believing yet that her disguise had fooled him so completely; but Kerk said nothing else, he just stood there, the sunlight playing off his dark curls, and at length Paragrin smiled. Standing a little taller, she offered him her hand. "I'm called . . ." she began again, "Gret."

"A name at last! Well, you're fine to meet, Gret." He took her hand and shook it heartily. "I'm Kerk, and my Partner here is my big brother, Cam."

Having decided long ago that Cam bore no more resemblance to his spirited brother than she did to Strap, Paragrin only glanced at the tall young man and nodded. "You're awfully fine to meet as well," she added, turning to Kerk.

"It's unusual for a Colonist to stray this far from the Melde, isn't it?" said Cam.

"Who said I was from the Melde?"

"Well," Cam replied, giving her an odd look, "you're not from Lexterre, and unless more people have rebelled against Trag in the ten years we've been gone, there isn't anywhere *else* to go."

Paragrin colored. "I know. Of course I come from the Colony. I just didn't like your tone, that's all."

"He didn't mean anything," Kerk put in, clapping her on the back. "Come, Gret, we were about to eat lunch. I have apples. Plenty for all!" He took three from the pouch he had slung across his shoulder, and tossed one to his brother and to Paragrin before throwing himself down on the grass, face to the sun, and biting into his own. Paragrin glanced across to the older

18

boy, uncertain, then sank down beside Kerk. Cam, after a moment, did the same.

"So, Gret," said Kerk. "What are you doing here? Spying on Lexterre?"

"No," she said quickly, "I'm just . . . on a journey."

"To Lexterre?"

"No, just around."

"Why?"

"Because I want to. Isn't that a good enough reason?" Cam was watching her, and she shifted her position so that he couldn't see her face.

"It's good enough for me," said Kerk.

"After all, I might ask you the same question," she returned. "What are you doing away from the village?"

Kerk sat up and grinned. "Adventure!" he said. "At least, that's my reason. Cam, here, being a dull sort, merely wants to *observe* the Melde."

"You're going to the Melde?"

Kerk nodded.

"Why, that's wonderful! That's where I'm going—back home. I'll go with you."

"Will you?" said Kerk.

"Well," she faltered, "if you'll let me."

"I don't know. Do you think we should let Little Gret tag along, Partner?"

"This was going to be a time for *us*," his brother replied.

"You're right. We'd have to change our plan to include him." Kerk put on a thoughtful expression. "What makes you think you're good enough for all that trouble, Little Gret?"

19

"Don't call me that. And I'm good enough for any-one."

"You are, are you? Pretty feisty for such a little fellow. Just how old are you? Too young for whiskers, anyway," he teased, and reached out to feel her face.

Paragrin pulled back, alarmed, her hand at her blade.

"Oho!" Kerk cried. "You're going to prove your worth by doing battle! Good for you. But none of this knife business. A real man uses his fists in a fight."

"Oh," she said, and after a moment's hesitation, took her hand from the weapon.

"All right, now you're ready to take anyone on. Cam, get up there and have a go at Little Gret."

"Have a go at him?" said Cam, surprised.

"Come on, Partner, afraid he'll whip you?"

"I just don't like to fight," his brother returned. "You know that."

Paragrin rolled her eyes. Why, she made a better boy than *he* did. She wasn't scared of fighting and would do it if Kerk wanted her to. She had always wondered what it would be like to grapple with someone anyway, and now she had her chance. "Come on," she said, "what are you afraid of?" and did a dance in front of him, jabbing her fists at the air.

"There you go, Little Gret!" Kerk laughed. "Go on, Cam! You have your honor to defend."

Cam looked from one eager face to the other and sighed. "I don't know why you want me to do this," he said to Kerk.

"Because it's fun!"

"Fun. Well, all I have to do is get him down once, right?"

20

"That's right."

"If you can do it," Paragrin added, and jabbed the air again.

"All right, but only once," Cam conceded, and throwing aside his apple core, he rose to his feet.

Kerk cheered.

"Now I'm not going to hurt you," Cam assured her. "Just one quick—"

"GO!" Kerk cried, and before Cam could finish his sentence, Paragrin shot out at him. Startled, he raised his arms to defend himself and stumbled backward. The next moment he was flat on the ground, defeated by an ill-placed rock, while Paragrin stood above him glowing in triumph.

Kerk howled. "Whoa! Little Gret's a wild bear! He got you, Partner."

Cam reddened. "That wasn't fair," he said, picking himself up. "I wasn't ready."

"I'll fight you again!" Paragrin cried, attacking the air with a new vengeance. How wonderful all of this was! How glorious a boy's life. "I can fight anyone," she said gleefully.

Kerk smiled. "All right, Little Gret, someone's got to defend the family honor. I'll fight you."

"You?"

"You said anyone."

Paragrin paused. "Why not?" she said at last. If she could beat one boy, she could beat another. Today, she felt invincible.

But Kerk, she soon found, knew better how to block her frenzied punches. He stopped the second match short by delivering such a substantial blow that she was sent tumbling down the riverbank and halfway into the water.

"You didn't have to hit him so hard," said Cam, though he watched with a certain amount of satisfaction as Paragrin struggled to pull herself back onto land. "Why don't you just tell him that we wanted this journey to ourselves?"

"But Cam, this little fellow's so funny," Kerk returned. "He's got a lot of spirit." And with that, he skipped down the embankment and helped her out of the water. "You still want to come with me, Little Gret?"

She nodded, dazed.

"Well then, come on!" He clapped his hands. "Let's get this journey started."

Paragrin and Cam each reached for the bows they had left on the ground, and their eyes met. Cam looked at her and turned away, but Paragrin didn't care; Kerk had welcomed her. She quickly fell in behind him, and Cam, shaking his head, brought up the rear.

For the rest of the day, Paragrin enjoyed her exile immensely. Becoming a boy, she was soon convinced, was the smartest thing she had ever done. In what other way could she have had such freedom, and traveled so with Kerk, side by side? He talked at her constantly, and in the course of the afternoon taught her how to shinny up trees, turn somersaults, and skip stones on the surface of the River. Paragrin was delighted to discover she could perform all these new and wonderful tricks; and Kerk, sensing early on the stranger's admiration for him, took every opportunity to justify the idolatry.

But at night, when she sat apart from the boys, too breathless to sleep, Paragrin began to wonder if she could really keep her identity safe during these days of close companionship. Already she had had to excuse herself—awkwardly—to seek relief behind a bush, and once or twice she had forgotten to keep her voice low and her step heavy. But then, as she looked down at Kerk, with his merry grin dissolved into the faintest of smiles, and his thick dark lashes and unruly tufts of hair lying quiet against his tanned face, she saw in his handsome form such a sweet vulnerability that she quickly forgot she had ever had misgivings.

4

When Paragrin woke in the morning, the boys were already up and returning, their catch in hand, from spear fishing in the River.

"Breakfast time," said Kerk, throwing the trout to the ground in front of her. "If you had slept any later, you'd have missed it."

Paragrin stared down at the fish, dismayed. "I'm sorry," she said, "but I'm afraid I'm not going to be very good at cooking."

"Oh, that's all right, Little Gret," said Kerk. "Where we come from, men don't even learn about that."

She looked at him dumbly for a second, then smiled. "So what happens when there aren't any women nearby?" she asked.

"*I* cook," said Cam, and he knelt by the trout to skin them.

24

"Oh. Well, what do you do, just fling them on the flame, and see what works?"

"He can do better than that," Kerk returned. "He can make them taste good. Now come on, Little Gret, let's see about starting the fire."

Kerk set out to find kindling, but Paragrin hesitated, watching Cam as he readied the fish for eating. "You really seem to know what you're doing," she said.

Cam laughed. "I do. I enjoy it."

"You enjoy it?" said Paragrin, surprised.

"Yes!"

She stared at him. "Isn't that kind of peculiar?"

Cam's knife paused on the meat, and he was silent for a moment. "I suppose that all depends on what you think is peculiar," he said at last, and without meeting her eyes, returned briskly to his work.

After the three of them had enjoyed a delicious break-fast—flavored with wild spices and herbs that Cam had collected from the forest—they set out again down the riverbank. Paragrin started her journey as eagerly as she had the day before, but by afternoon the long hike took its toll on her. She lagged behind, and when, at last, the brothers decided to make camp for the night, she flung herself to the ground, resentful, and thought how unfair it was that Strap had never trained her to use her muscles.

Exhausted, she closed her eyes, and when a shout from Kerk roused her a minute later, she sat up, looked across at him drowsily—and dropped her jaw. "Great Maker!" she whispered.

"We're going swimming. Come on!" Kerk called.

Paragrin blinked and looked again. Yes. He and his brother were standing side by side on the riverbank—their clothes discarded behind them—naked. Although every instinct that Aridda had tried to instill in her told Paragrin to avert her eyes immediately, she couldn't resist staring at the strange figures before her. Never had she seen such a sight! She chewed her lip nervously, and decided that her body, as unfeminine as she had thought it, had no chance of passing for the same type as those that stood before her. Her breasts and hips felt larger then, and she twitched uncomfortably in her clothes.

"Let's go!" said Kerk. "What do you wait for?"

"We—we don't do that in the Melde," she said, trying to concentrate on his face.

The boys exchanged looks. "Awfully modest, aren't you?" said Kerk.

"It's not modesty," she insisted, "it's just considered rude where I come from."

Kerk grinned, and began to walk toward her. "Now come, Little Gret, don't be afraid."

Paragrin got to her feet. "I'm not afraid. Stay away."

His grin broadened. "You *are* afraid, aren't you?"

"Kerk," said Cam, "why don't you leave him alone?"

But Kerk, deaf to all, suddenly swung out his hand to grab her jacket. Horrified, Paragrin leaped back, whipping the knife from her belt. She lashed out at him, and the sharp blade just narrowly missed his arm. Kerk retreated, the laughter gone from his eyes.

"Have it your way then," he said at last, and turning, dove into the water.

Cam paused on the bank, watching her. "Are you all right?" he asked.

"Of course I am!" Paragrin snapped. The last thing she wanted was sympathy from him. The incident had been embarrassing enough.

She stayed up on the bank, miserable, while the boys swam; and when they finally came out again, she didn't even look at Kerk, afraid of the reproach in his eyes. But Kerk didn't mention the knife again, and as soon as he was dressed, he squatted down in front of her and smiled.

"Ho, Little Gret. Want to go hunting?" he asked.

Paragrin looked up, incredulous.

"Well, you have that fancy bow," he continued. "You must be pretty good—not as good as me, I'm sure, but there's a better chance of hitting game if two of us go. Are you willing?"

"Yes!" said Paragrin. "Just a moment; I'll get my arrows." She sprang to her feet.

"You know, I could have gone with you," said Cam, handing Kerk his bow. "Gret could try his hand at cooking."

Kerk looked at his brother, puzzled. "But I thought you didn't really like to hunt," he said.

Cam crossed his arms firmly in front of him. "Well," he returned, shooting a quick glance at Paragrin, "I don't, really, I just wanted you to know that I *could* hunt instead of cook if I wanted to. I'm pretty good with an arrow."

Kerk stared at him. "I know," he said. "Did I ever say you weren't?"

"No," Cam assured him. "I just . . . I just wanted it *said*, that's all. Now go on and do your hunting, and the fire will be ready when you come back." And without meeting their eyes again, he set off on his own to collect wood.

"Sometimes he really baffles me," said Kerk, frowning, and Paragrin, forcing her gaze away from Cam, followed Kerk into the woods.

That night, after a fine dinner of roasted rabbit—shot by Paragrin's arrow—the companions sat by the River and talked, for the air was still hot, and no one felt like sleeping. At first the topics were general enough, but then Kerk introduced a subject that made Paragrin lean closer.

He went on for some time, while she listened, astounded, about the number of young women he had coupled with. She was shocked, not only that he had gone against Strap's strict teachings about celibacy before Joining, but also that there had been girls, girls whom she *knew*, who were willing parties to his actions. Ellagette, as she suspected, turned out to be the popular choice.

"She *is* beautiful," Paragrin sighed.

"How do you know?" said Kerk, turning on her.

Paragrin looked up, startled. "Oh, I just assumed, the way you described her and all."

Kerk smiled. "Well, you're right. She is beautiful—the most beautiful of all the village girls, don't you think, Partner?"

"Oh, probably," he said, "although Viletta is pretty."

28

"No, she isn't. If anyone, Amalee comes closest to Ellagette," said Kerk.

"If you like short girls," Cam put in. "I think Viletta and probably Joyanna are the prettiest."

Paragrin looked from one boy to the other, hopeful, but the conversation ended there, with Kerk muttering something about his brother's taste in women and flopping out on the grass. She waited for a moment, debating, then gave in to her curiosity and asked—as casually as she could feign—what ranking their leader's sister might have. "I don't know her name," she said.

"Her name's Paragrin," said Cam.

"Oh, her," Kerk yawned. "Well, she's not much to look at. She's just not the kind you notice much."

"Ahh," she said.

"Enough talk of women," he declared. "Thinking about Ellagette has got me all hot again." He closed his eyes. "Good night!"

"Good night," Paragrin mumbled, and turned away.

It was then that she noticed Cam staring at her, his eyes filled with a strange, confused light. She caught her breath, deeply repentant, and cursed herself for mentioning her name. But in the next moment the light in his eyes dimmed, and shrugging, he too lay down to sleep.

Paragrin breathed a little easier then, though she moved apart from the boys anyway, and worried what would happen if they did come to discover her secret. Their behavior would undoubtedly change, and not for the better, she decided, so she vowed to be more careful; especially, she was realizing, around Cam.

5

The next day turned cold—unusually so for autumn—and Cam and Paragrin quickened their pace, hugging themselves as they walked. But Kerk seemed unaffected by the change in weather and even braved the River for an afternoon swim, while the others sat warming their hands by a fire.

"Doesn't he ever get cold or tired or depressed?" Paragrin muttered, holding her palms to the blaze.

"Not often," said Cam, and laughed.

The two of them fell silent then, lost in their private thoughts, until, with her recollections of the Melde looming large in her mind, Paragrin began to sing a song that she had learned as a child there, long ago:

"Beneath the fair Green Mountains,
  Along the River Melde,

The children of the Maker,
Their . . . their . . ."

Here she faltered, time dimming her memory of the
words. Then another voice, low and gentle, added:

". . . their perfect home beheld;
        Lands and waters,
        Sons and daughters,
Their perfect home beheld."

Paragrin looked at Cam in surprise. He seemed a little
surprised himself, and without returning her gaze, said,
"I just think it's an interesting song, that's all."
        She stared at him. "You have a very nice voice,"
she said finally. "Do you know any more of the words?"
        "Some."
        "Would you sing them?"
        Cam turned to her. "You *want* me to sing them?"
        "Yes, please!"
        He hesitated, glancing across to Kerk, but seeing his
brother lost in the pleasures of the swim, relaxed.
"Well," he said at last, "I suppose it's all right, here—"
and closing his eyes, he took a deep breath and began
again, his voice rising with confidence.

"Oh, praise the love of Essai,
    For such an earth to dwell;
    We'll ever stay and prosper here,
    And serve our Maker well;
        Lands and waters,
        Sons and daughters,
    And serve our Maker well."

31

He opened his eyes and smiled.

"Why, that's marvelous!" Paragrin cried. "You're really good!"

"What was that?" demanded Kerk, who had just come from the water, his jacket wrapped around him like a blanket.

"Cam was singing," the girl exclaimed. "His voice is beautiful!"

"Singing? Oh, Partner . . ."

Cam's smile faded.

"The cooking's one thing," said Kerk, "we have to eat; but you know how much I hate it when you sing." He frowned and took up the rest of his clothes.

Paragrin looked from one boy to the other, confused. "But he has a beautiful voice," she protested, turning to Kerk.

"I wouldn't know about *that*," said Kerk, "but if he does, then all the more reason to keep it quiet. Where we come from, Little Gret, men aren't supposed to do things like this. For a man to sing is like announcing he's soft, or something." He sat down beside her to pull on his boots. "You understand about that, don't you?"

"I suppose," said Paragrin, and wondered that she had never really thought about Strap's restrictions for boys. Not being able to sing never seemed as terrible as not being able to hunt. Still . . . it didn't seem right, somehow, for Cam to be chastised for singing so wonderfully. She glanced across at him, but he looked away.

"Now as I figure it," said Kerk, standing and shaking the water from his hair, "if we keep moving for the rest of the day, we'll get to the city by nightfall."

"In the dark?" said Cam.

"Yes. Why not?"

"Well, we don't know our way around anymore, Kerk. We could get lost, or separated."

"Oh, rot. Nothing's going to happen. Besides, if it *has* changed that much since we left—which I doubt—we still have Little Gret here to show us around."

Paragrin smiled feebly.

"Well, I don't know. Look at the sky, Kerk, it's going to rain, maybe even storm, and it might make more sense to wait it out in the woods, instead of traveling anymore today. That way we could get a fresh start in the morning."

"It'll go fine, Partner, you'll see," Kerk assured him. "If it does rain, then we can get proper shelter in the city—maybe in the arms of a woman. They're not as modest as in Lexterre, you know." He grinned.

Cam sighed and relented, but he wasn't the only one with worries. The more she thought of their arrival, the more apprehensive Paragrin became. It wasn't so much that she feared the Colony, but that she felt nervous about striking out on her own again. The boys' companionship had grown too comfortable for her, and she was saddened to think that soon she would lose them forever; for whatever happened during the next few days, she knew she wouldn't be going back with them to Lexterre. This new place—this old place—was going to be her home.

All day the travelers walked toward the city. The Green Mountains, covered with pines, stretched upward now on both sides of the River and stood huge and ominous against the dark sky. But the rain held off, and Kerk led them on, defiantly.

And then, just as the pale light of day began to fade, Kerk came bounding back from a scouting expedition to say that they were there. He had heard sounds, *people* sounds. Paragrin's fingers strayed to the Amulet beneath her jacket for support, and resigned, she followed the brothers forward to the Colony.

6

How strange it was, suddenly, to have the evening so full of people; and not just their bodies, but their noises as well. The screams, scuffles, and scraps of conversation in the old city filled Paragrin's ears as she passed by the first row of riverside houses and into the central court. What an alarming thing—to see, at one glance, a larger assemblage than your entire town's population, so many different faces and figures, pushing past you, talking over you, completely oblivious to your existence.

Paragrin was astounded, and stopped in her tracks to stare. She had not remembered the Melde as being so crowded or so confusing. The central court had been wide and open in her time, and now three large buildings made of wood and mud squatted there, scarring the lawn and walkways. The houses surrounding the yard had worsened too; the stones from their walls tumbled out into the alleys. And the people! What was it about their faces, the way they walked, that made them seem so sad, so defeated? People in Lexterre weren't like this. Paragrin shuddered, and wondered if the Colony had really changed since she'd left, or if it had always been this way, and she had just been too young to notice.

"What's wrong with you?" came a voice, and she turned to find herself confronted by a small gang of boys, each of them wearing a soiled red kerchief tied around his neck. The one in front was the biggest, just an inch or so shorter than she was, and he grinned at her, revealing an incomplete row of teeth.

"Nothing's wrong," she said.

"Wait a bit," the boy insisted, grabbing her arm. "Whose troop you in?"

"Troop? Nobody's troop. Let go of me."

"Nobody's?" sneered the boy. "What are you, a fluff?"

She frowned, and pushed his hand away.

"Fluff!" the boy cried after her. "Come on back, and I'll—"

Paragrin ignored him and went to catch up with Kerk. She made her way through the people to hold on to his sleeve, and relaxed—until he turned around—for it wasn't Kerk at all, but a stranger.

"What do you think you're doing?" the man said, knocking her hand, "trying to steal my blade?"

"No," Paragrin breathed, "I'm sorry, I thought—"

"You thought wrong. Get out of here, before I—"

She didn't wait for the end of his threat to appease

him. She turned and went as fast as she could in the other direction, scouring the crowded court for Kerk. But she found him nowhere; he was gone, and Cam with him. She was alone.

Paragrin clenched her fists. "Now, it's all right," she told herself, "I expected this"; but she had not expected it so soon. Nervously she pulled at her jacket, debating what to do, when her fingers brushed against the Oval. The Amulet . . . and her fear fell away in that moment. She spun about, and tried to recall where the little stone house had been. She pushed her way through the people, walking, then running around the length of the court, searching; yet for all her effort she found nothing, not even a marking in the earth to show where it once had stood.

Again, the panic rose within her. "This doesn't mean anything," she swore to herself. "Just because it's gone doesn't mean *she* is. All I have to do is ask someone."

But who to ask? Most of the people around her looked unreceptive, and she hung back until she remembered a different sort of person who might be able to help her. Beyond the Colony streets and beside the planting fields stood an old barn made of stone, which had been used, in better times, for storing surplus food. Yet when Paragrin had been a child, a band of women had lived in its empty shell—strange women who kept apart from the rest of the city. People had told her to stay away from them, that they were eccentric; but to a child, the women had seemed more mysterious than dangerous, as if they knew secrets no one else did. If her mother had gone or had been sent somewhere, perhaps the old barn would hold the answers—and maybe even the woman herself.

Heartened, she left the court behind her and passed through to the broken rows of smaller houses that surrounded it. She was eyed by gangs of dirty children as she moved along the darkening streets, and they called out to her, but Paragrin only quickened her pace; and then, at last, when she had reached the end of the settlement, there was the barn before her. She ran toward it, hopeful, yet as she drew closer and saw the faces of the women cooking over the fires, she slowed, hesitant, feeling the Amulet again for support.

"What do you come for, boy?" demanded one of the women. She was tall and looked down at Paragrin proudly, though her face and clothes were worn. "If it's food, go to your own fires."

"Hold off, Assandra," came a voice, and a wizened old creature shot up from the stump where she had been sitting. "He's come to *trade* for food, haven't you, boy? I'll trade meat for those warm boots you got."

"No, I don't want to trade anything," said the girl, "and I don't want to take your food." She glanced about at the women, trying to find in their haggard forms some spark of familiarity. But there was none.

"What, then?" said a third woman. "If it's a bit of adventure, you've come to the wrong place. You'll find ones more willing back at the tavern."

"No, I—I don't want *that*," Paragrin stammered. "I just wanted to ask a question about a woman . . . a woman that I knew once."

"You couldn't have known too many at your age,"

returned Assandra dryly, and the people around her laughed. The other women drew in closer to watch the scene, and Paragrin stepped back, her eyes shifting uncomfortably from face to face.

"I knew her ten years ago. She was . . . She was very beautiful."

"Beautiful? I'm sure she *was*!" called the third woman, and the crowd grinned at the sport and waited for more.

"She was kept in a little stone house," Paragrin persisted, "at the edge of the court." And suddenly, the people around her fell silent.

"Tempira!" whispered the crone, her eyes wide. "You mean Tempira . . . ah, she was beautiful. I remember."

Paragrin's heart leaped. "Where is she, then? Is she here?"

The old woman started. "Here? Great Maker, child, what do you mean?"

"I mean, does she *live* here!"

"She's dead," said Assandra, her gaze turned cold. "Of course she's dead."

Paragrin stared back at her. "No. No, it can't be!"

"Long time now," said the crone, "almost ten years. Didn't you know? It was horrible sad, what he did to her. She was so strong before she came here."

"She was strong right until the end," said Assandra, her gaze not moving from Paragrin's face, "until Trag finally killed her."

Paragrin, unable to keep down her tears, backed away.

"Why did you come here?" the third woman demanded. "Why should you care what happened to her?"

"You won't tell Trag what we've said, will you, boy?"

39

pleaded the old woman. "It was you who asked. Why did you come? Who *are* you, anyway?"

But Paragrin answered none of their questions. She turned and ran, ran until the women and their fires were out of sight; and then, sinking down on the earth, she drew the Amulet out from her jacket and, clutching it to her heart, wept.

7

After the tears had passed, Paragrin knew what she had to do: return to Lexterre with the boys and beg Strap to forgive her. She had been wrong, very wrong, in giving him reason to banish her in the first place; Strap, who had saved her from this wretched, hateful settlement. If Lexterre was bad, the Melde was evil, and given a choice, she would go home; even if it meant giving in to her brother's rule, she would do it now.

She rose to her feet, shivering, and blinked at the eerie brightness shining over the Colony. The central torches had been lit, and she walked slowly back through the dark streets toward the glow. The smell of ale—an odor not often breathed in Lexterre—grew strong as she neared the court, and the raucous noise of the people stung her ears; yet she pressed on, and within

41

minutes was back where she had started.

But how different the court looked from her first view in the twilight! Now the fire from the torches, standing out against the deep blackness of the night, transformed the familiar to the fantastic, and sent crazy lights and shadows darting through the square. Shapes of buildings and people changed, and as Paragrin, suddenly swept up into the current of the crowd, tried in vain to find something, anything, that she could recognize, the despair came at last to claim her. The loneliness and the fear rose up, more fierce than ever, and she felt herself about to faint when a face loomed up in front of her, and she gasped.

"Cam!"

"Gret!"

And in the impulsive relief of the moment, they embraced.

When Paragrin, feeling foolish, began to pull away, Cam held fast to her hand. "Great Maker, don't let go," he said, "that's all we need, to get separated again. Come on." And he led her to stand more safely by a house. "I can't tell you what a nightmare this has been," he said, squinting into the torchlight. "How can you take living here?"

"I don't—" she began, but stopped herself. "I don't like it much myself," she finished after a moment. "Where's your brother?"

"I was hoping you knew. I lost sight of him about half an hour ago. I—"

"Rot! Get out of my way, will you?" The travelers turned, and found an old man trying to force his walking

42

stick between them. Cam's eyes widened, and he moved aside.

"We couldn't see you coming in the dark, my leader," he said, giving a quick bow. "I'm sorry."

"Rot again," the old man swore. "This whole place has gone to seed. In my day, a man could—" He faltered. The light from the torches played over Paragrin's face. "A man could . . ." he began again, but was struck dumb, staring.

"Is there something wrong?" asked Cam.

The man didn't answer. He was silent, gaping, but then, as if he couldn't quite believe what he was seeing, he leaned closer to Paragrin and squinted for a better look.

"Augh!" he cried.

The suddenness of this exclamation made Cam and Paragrin jump, but not as far as the old man. An instant after his cry, he turned and bolted, disappearing into the darkness.

"Well, that was strange," said Paragrin.

"What did you do to him?" Cam asked, turning on her.

"Nothing! I don't even know who he is."

"What do you mean, you don't know? That was the old leader; Trag's father."

"That was Ram?" asked the girl, uncertain.

"Of course that was Ram!" Cam cried. "How could you not know that if you live here? Even I know that!"

"Don't shout at me," Paragrin countered. "What does it matter what I know and what I don't know?"

Cam was silent, watching her.

Paragrin frowned. "Let's just try to find Kerk, all right?"

"All right," said the young man at last. "I was going to look in the tavern next."

"The tavern? Fine, then let's go," and she started off.

"Gret," said Cam quietly, taking her arm, "it's this way—" and he turned her to face the first squat building in the center.

"I know it," she muttered, and shaking off his arm, forged across the square.

When they entered the low, sprawling room, it was hot with torches and bodies. The odor of ale hung stagnant in the air.

"How are we going to find him in this mob?" sighed Paragrin.

"I don't know. It looks hopeless," Cam agreed, and then he brightened. "Wait! Did you hear that?"

"Hear what?"

"That was Kerk's whoop! I know it was."

"His what?"

"His whoop! He must be winning at something. I've heard him use that victory cry a thousand times. Come on!"

"Cam, how can you be sure that—"

"It came from over there," he insisted, and plunged into the crowd.

Paragrin followed, unconvinced, but when they emerged again from the throng, Kerk was in front of them, sitting at a greasy table in a corner with five other men.

"Oh, Kerk, I knew that had to be you!" Cam exclaimed. "You don't know how long I've been searching this awful city."

Kerk turned from the table and looked up. "Oh, hi. What do you want? I have to get back to the game."

"Oh. Well, I was just wondering if you wanted to go off for the night."

"You mean off from the Colony?"

"Well, yes."

"What for? I just got here. What's the matter? Why aren't you out there *observing?*"

"I think I've seen enough," said Cam.

Kerk made a face. "Do what you want. I'll meet up with you later. Much later."

"What exactly are you doing?" asked Paragrin, eying the other men uneasily.

"Gambling!" said Kerk, and grinned. "It's fine! We're tossing these dried nuts in the basket, see, and betting which one will end up in the center. They're all differently marked, and—"

"You playing or explaining?" demanded an older man at the table. He made Paragrin particularly uneasy. He didn't sit as tall as the others, but he was thickly built, and had a full red beard that burst from his chin. When the torch set into the wall behind him flickered, Paragrin suddenly became aware of a wolf tail pinned to his shirt. She remembered those from before—they were the uniform of her father's soldiers. Glancing about her, she noticed that most of the men in the tavern wore the tails, and she pulled in a little closer to Cam.

"Oh, quiet up," Kerk said to the player. "You're

45

just angry I've won three of your blades, that's all."

"Kerk, when do you think you'll—" Cam began.

"Talk to you later, Partner," he said, his dark eyes intent, as the bearded man threw the nuts into the basket. Cam sighed, and he and Paragrin started back toward the door. Kerk whooped in delight as he won again, and the companions, discouraged, went outside to wait.

"He's never going to leave," muttered Paragrin, as she leaned against the side of the tavern, "unless we're lucky, and he starts to lose."

A woman with her blouse pulled down around her shoulders ambled out of the tavern door and her gaze fell on Cam. She paused, her fingers twirling slowly in her unkempt hair.

"Let's get away from here," said Paragrin, and she was just reaching for his arm when the woman suddenly dropped to her knees before them.

"What's wrong?" asked Cam, bending toward her, but then all at once a stroke of lightning ripped through the sky, and he fell back, clutching at Paragrin's arm. There coming toward them was a huge, ungainly man, his towering figure lit for a second by the lightning's glare. Everyone in the court sank to their knees, so Cam did the same; but the sight of her father stunned Paragrin, and she stayed as she was, staring, until Cam pulled her down beside him.

"What do you think you're doing?" he hissed. "You know who *that* is, don't you?"

Paragrin knew; and her eyes, deep with hate as the women's words rushed back to her, held him still.

Yet Trag cared not what emotions he was causing.

46

The great Ruler of the Melde cared for nothing then except the tavern, and with his massive bearskin cape draped about his shoulders, and his father Ram close at his heels, he lumbered through the passive crowd, his powerful arms swinging at his sides. Cam glanced up, and was just as impressed and horrified by the sight of the Rectangular Amulet against his mighty chest as he had been in his boyhood. Trag wore the iron defiantly—as a reminder—and unchallenged, he walked into the tavern.

The instant after he stepped through the door, the noisy brawl of the room ceased, and the men and women, deserting their drink and games, bowed down to him— all except for one. A triumphant whoop rang unchecked through the room, and out over the silent square.

Cam shuddered.

Pulled out of his gloomy meditation, the Ruler looked down, surprised, to see who had dared to defy him.

Kerk looked up himself to see why the room had grown so quiet, and his smile faded.

"Well," Trag muttered, "another rebel. How tiresome." He glanced to the table, and the man with the red beard nodded.

Kerk slowly rose to his feet, looking about warily at the soldiers, who seemed, suddenly, to be everywhere. "I'm not a rebel," he said. "I'm from Lexterre."

"Are you really?" said Trag. "How unexpected. But then you're just a rebel of another sort, aren't you, my buck?"

Cam tried to enter the tavern, but a soldier blocked his way with a spear. "You can't go in," said the man, "but don't worry. The action'll end up out here. It always does."

"Now if you bend like the others," said the Ruler, "perhaps I'll forget your impudence."

"I don't have to bow to you," Kerk countered. "That's why I left the Melde in the first place."

"It's a pity you came back, then, isn't it?" said Trag quietly, and motioned to his men.

Kerk turned and grabbed a blade from the table, but the man behind him caught his wrist, and while two other soldiers threw him against the wall, the red beard forced the knife from his grasp.

"Let me go!" Kerk shouted, but they didn't listen. Kerk doubled over as he was hit once, twice, by the soldiers.

"Kerk!" Cam cried, and tried again to go to him, but the guard knocked him away. Paragrin stood apart, too paralyzed with dread to move.

The next moment, four of the men hoisted Kerk into the air and, at Trag's command, flung him out in the court. He landed hard, in a twist of limbs, and painfully he tried to raise himself from the dirt before his arms buckled beneath him, and he collapsed again, silent.

At Trag's reappearance, the people in the courtyard drew back. The torchlight played across them, one sad and angry face after another illuminated and then lost again in the darkness.

Cam, kneeling at his brother's side, turned on Trag hotly. "What right had you to do this?" he said. "Kerk didn't do anything to you!"

"He was insolent," the Ruler returned. Ram, back in the tavern, came to stand by the doorway and watch, his shrewish eyes narrowing as he recognized Cam. "And you, my buck," added Trag, "are dangerously close to being the same."

So filled with indignation that he shook, Cam got to his feet.

"Before you do anything foolish," the Ruler said with a smile, "I suggest you take your friend and go back where you came from."

"You're a savage," Cam breathed, and Trag struck him across the face.

"No!" Paragrin yelled, breaking from her stupor at last, and she flung herself at Trag, beating at him with her fists.

He seized her arms to stay the attack, but she bit his hand when she could do no more, and with a yelp he thrust her arms behind her back; the collar laces of her jacket strained and broke apart with the force, showing a glimmer of iron beneath.

Ram's eyes widened.

"I hate you!" Paragrin cried, struggling in his hold. "You *murderer!*"

Another bolt of lightning lit the court, and Trag suddenly saw before him a defiant face so strange and yet so familiar that an agonizing memory of another face rose up to torment him. He released her instantly.

"Dear Essai," he gasped. "Tempira!"

A clap of thunder exploded above the Colony, and torrents of rain and sleet came crashing down upon them. People shrieked, running for shelter, and the torches sizzled and went out, leaving the court in blackness.

"Don't let her get away!" Ram shouted. "She's got it! Find her. *Find her!*"

But Cam had risen and taken Paragrin's hand. Together they got Kerk to his feet and, with their arms locked around him, darted away into the darkness.

"Tempira! Come back!" Trag screamed, blind and deafened by the fury of the storm. He spun around, his big arms flailing about helplessly.

But it was useless. The three companions had fled the city and were gone, and the great Ruler, sinking down to his knees in wretched desolation, let out a wail of despair.

He had lost her. Again.

8

Far into the woods the travelers ran, with the tempest raging on around them. Sometimes the lightning would show their way through the tangle of trees, but more often it didn't, and when their legs could carry them no further, they fell, bruised and exhausted.

"Rot him," Kerk swore between gasps. "He had no right!"

Paragrin staggered to her feet and, tying her collar close again, went to Kerk. He had regained his senses early in their flight, yet she could tell from his movements that he was still hurting. She reached out, but he knocked her hand away.

"Don't you treat me like a fluff, Little Gret!" he snapped. "I can take care of myself," and he turned over onto the leaves.

"I was only trying to help," she retorted, but Cam held up his hand.

"Let him try to sleep," he said, "that's the best thing." He mopped his face with a sleeve. "My Maker, what a night! I don't think I've run so fast in all my life." He paused. "Are you all right?"

"I suppose so," said Paragrin, and fended off a sudden shower of water that fell through the branches.

"Do you want to talk about what happened?" he asked quietly.

She turned and peered at him through the dark. "No," she said decisively, and went off to sit by herself.

Back at the Melde, Ram rushed from the tavern door and fell upon his son. "Trag, you fool, get up!" he cried. "It's got away!"

The Ruler was still bent upon the muddied earth, and while the sleet danced madly around him, he turned a pale face to his father. "I don't understand," he said, "that girl . . . it all came back to me in one blow . . . all the pain."

"Forget the pain!" shouted the old man, and he wrapped his wrinkled hands around Trag's shoulders to shake him. "Blast, it wasn't the girl that reminded you of Tempira, it was the Amulet. That girl has the other one. I saw it!"

"The Oval Amulet?" Trag breathed.

"Yes! Forty years it's been out of our sight, and you lose it again in one night. Get up, you oaf, now! Send out the men to find it!"

"But the girl," said Trag, rising to his feet, "she looked so much like—"

52

"Blast Tempira! Find the Oval!"

"You and that Oval," Trag snarled, seizing the old man by the throat, "that's all you ever cared about."

"It's all *she* cared about!" squeaked Ram. "Never the Melde. Never you! Remember the pain!"

Another stroke of lightning crackled above them, and the sleet, more thick than ever, beat down against their faces.

His grip loosened on his father's neck. "I do remember," said Trag, "her conceit, her unyielding pride . . ."

"She hated you," said Ram.

"I hated her more," returned the Ruler, and tightened his grip again, as if to show how much.

"Then avenge yourself before it's too late!" Ram cried. "We're wasting time. We've got to find that Oval and keep it hidden, or else the lies of the past will come crashing down on us both like thunder!"

"No, they won't," said Trag, shoving Ram away. "Storm or no, my men will find the girl and the Oval— and I'll do better than keep it, old man; Great Maker, I'll have her and that wretched thing destroyed!"

Under the trembling forest trees, where the wind had moaned now for hours in the branches, Paragrin paced, her fingers nervously playing with the iron beneath the cloth. Images of her father kept looming up in front of her in the dark: his sneering expression turning fearful, again and again, while her mother's name, said in his foul breath, rang in her ears. It was all so hateful, so confusing. She looked to the sleeping boys for comfort, yet even there Trag had taken his toll; not only

53

on Kerk, but on Cam as well. As the lightning's blaze
lit the wood, she saw for the first time the gash on his
cheek where Trag had struck him. Her heart went out
then, and she was sorry she hadn't offered her help to
him, instead of to Kerk.

And then she heard a noise.

It wasn't a noise like the wind or the water made; it
was a different sort altogether—a *people* noise—and close
by. Paragrin dropped to the ground, listening.

"This cursed rain," came a voice.

"Quiet up. Just a bit longer, and we'll go back," said
a second.

"And if none of the other fellows find her? He'll
get us all, you know it," said the first. "Besides, there'll
be a reward for the ones that bring her in. A big one,
I hear."

"I don't believe there even *is* a girl," said a third.
"The small one with the 'fire' in her eyes, he says. Mad-
ness . . ."

Paragrin's eyes widened. "Cam, wake up," she whispered. "Kerk!"

Kerk muttered in his sleep, and rolled over.

"What's the matter?" Cam whispered back.

"There're men in the woods," she said. "Soldiers."

Cam got up quickly and put his arm around his
brother. "Come on, Kerk," he said. "We have to go.
Now!" and he pulled on his sleeve.

Still thick with sleep, Kerk turned over on his back
and looked at him. "What're you doing?" he demanded
in a loud voice.

Cam's hand shot across his mouth—too late.

54

"Great Father! There they are!" cried the first man.

Paragrin gasped, and as Cam yanked a surprised Kerk to his feet, the three companions turned and bolted farther into the forest.

But the soldiers had their prize in view. They flew after Paragrin, weapons in hand, and the girl herself could only just stay ahead. She heard them crashing through the brush behind her, and glancing over her shoulder, she tripped over a tree root and fell sprawling to the ground.

"I've got her!" said the second man.

She scrambled up to see all three coming at her. They were only yards away, and she drew her blade for a useless fight, when suddenly a terrible boom filled the air. A bolt of lightning shot down to the roots of an oak that stood only inches apart from where she had fallen, and with a mighty crack, it split the tree in two. Paragrin screamed, but both halves of the severed tree trunk fell away from her and down upon the soldiers. She turned from their shrieks to find the brothers coming back for her, and together they fled from the kill and didn't stop that night until they were far, far away.

9

The morning finally came, gray and dreary. Trag emerged red eyed from the tavern, and cursed at the rain that still poured from the sky. One by one the troops of the Melde had hauled themselves home again, half drowned and empty-handed, and he had just finished treating the last few men to his mood. Jug in hand, he stumbled across the soggy court to his house at the head of the square, and throwing aside the bearskin that served as a door, went in.

"Trag! There you are," cried Ram, hurrying down the passage to meet him. "I was just coming to find you."

"Out of my way, old man," said Trag. "I'm in no mind for you."

"Listen to me, you stupid lout," said Ram, and blocked his way. Trag, his heavy boots dragging to a stop, low-

56

ered his sights slowly, inch by inch, until at last they fell on the low and spindly figure of his father. He smiled dangerously, and Ram, peering up at him, softened his glare, and took a step backward. "I've good news," he said, in a kinder voice.

Trag lumbered past him to the fire at the hearth. "What possible good could you have?" he said.

"While you were out, I was thinking," said Ram. "It came to me this morning. I know who that girl is."

Trag took a swig of ale. "Really?"

Ram followed him to the fire, his eyes glistening. "You thought she looked like Tempira. Well, earlier on, I thought she looked like . . . like *her-whom-I-will-not-name*."

The Ruler gave an unpleasant laugh, and spat some ale into the flames.

"It all makes sense," said Ram. "Don't you see? Everything, the Amulet, the face . . . it's your *daughter*!"

The jug paused at Trag's lips.

"Don't you remember? The only child you could get from Tempira? The one you cast aside because it wasn't a son?"

"Is there no end to that woman's treachery?" Trag cried, hurling the jug to the floor. "Even in her death, she sends that girl to finish what she started!"

"Yes," said the old man. "Somehow, she was able to pass the Oval on to her. How, I don't know, since Tempira was searched when you brought her here. She must have had it, though, hidden somewhere, rot her."

"And now the girl's come back to claim her rights," said Trag.

"You won't let her, will you, Son?"

"Of course not. But how am I to put an end to this unfortunate girl if I don't even know where she is?"

"But that's it," said Ram, pressing his bony fingers into Trag's arm. "That's my good news. We do know where she is . . . or where she will be, in three days."

Trag stared down at him. "Where?"

"Think!" said the old man. "Where did this daughter go, ten years before, hand in hand with her pious older brother?"

"Sweet Divine," breathed Trag. "Lexterre."

"Of course!"

"I've been wrong to send my men to the forest," said Trag, gazing at his father with a newfound regard. "She's gone back to the village."

"Tempira's not beat you yet, Son," said Ram.

"Great Maker, I'll not be beat!" cried Trag. "Klay! Hann!" he called to his men. "Rally the troops again," he commanded, "we're going to Lexterre!"

And Ram, tasting the victory already, sucked his teeth in anticipation.

Deep in the wood, the day grew colder. The rain spattered down through the dying leaves, and the companions wandered on, tired and hungry, yet finding no heartier meals than the nuts and berries that the wind had knocked to the forest floor. Kerk stopped assuring the others that he knew where he was going, and walked ahead in sullen silence. Paragrin, feeling every bit as cross as he did, followed a distance behind, not even caring anymore to engage his attentions. Cam tried to keep cheerful, but failed miserably in his attempt, and when the sky had finally turned from gray to black again, they were no better off than they had been before.

Kerk dragged himself off to a dry place among the trees and closed his eyes, while Paragrin sat brooding, sifting the leaves around her into little piles. Cam watched her for a minute or so, then came and sat down beside her.

"This is pretty," he said, picking up a bright-orange leaf she had discarded.

Paragrin shrugged.

"Are you afraid we won't find our way out?" he asked gently.

"I'm not afraid of anything," she returned, and was silent again.

Cam traced the veins of the leaf with his thumb. "Gret," he said at last, "why were we followed?"

"How should I know? I suppose Trag wanted to find us."

Cam twirled the stem in his hand. "I don't think he wanted to find all of us," he said. "I think he just wanted to find you."

She looked across at him warily.

"Do you know why that could be?" he asked.

"No."

"Do you know why he was so scared when he saw your face?"

"He wasn't scared."

"Yes, he was, and he called you—"

"I *know* what he called me. I don't know why. I don't know anything. Just leave me alone, all right?" She bowed her head, ending the conversation.

59

"All right," he said, rising, "but if you ever decide to know something, *Gret*"—and he placed the leaf carefully in her lap—"I'll be here"—and he went off to sleep.

Paragrin sat alone, unmoving, as the rain dripped down around her; then she curled up on the ground with her eyes on Cam, gazing at him until she fell asleep. She had been too tired and engrossed in her thoughts to notice the shrouded figure who had hovered for some time behind her, among the trees.

The stranger's bright eyes looked down tenderly upon the girl; then, with her long white cloak fluttering about her, she shimmered softly in the night and disappeared—and the rain, falling harder then, turned to snow.

10

"Oh, I don't believe it!"

Paragrin woke at Kerk's exclamation, and sat up, blinking. All about the forest, on the trees and on the ground, stood an inch of snow, and it came down still, floating through the branches.

"Get up, Partner, you'll love this," said Kerk, and knocked the ice from his brother's hair.

Cam's eyes fluttered open and widened. He rolled over onto his back, staring at the sky. "It's a little early for snow, isn't it?" he said.

"Is that all you can say?" Kerk cried. "It's not enough that we're lost and starving. Now we have to freeze, too!"

"I don't suppose we could make a fire," Paragrin said, looking doubtfully at the wet wood.

61

"Oh, Little Gret, don't be stupid."

"Now it's not going to do any good to snap at one another," said Cam, rising and brushing the snow from his clothes. "We'll just have to keep going, that's all."

"Where?"

Cam sighed. "I don't know. Does it matter?"

"At least we won't feel so cold if we move," said Paragrin.

"That's right!"

"Well," said Kerk, shoving his hands under his arms to warm them, "you two happies can lead the way, then. Obviously my leadership hasn't helped us much."

"No one blames you, Kerk," said Paragrin. "Go on. I've been following you for so long, I don't think I could do anything else."

After a moment, he smiled. "All right, Little Gret," Kerk said, "come on, then"—and he started off.

"That was a nice thing you did," said Cam, walking behind her. "I think he's felt a bit responsible for all this."

"I've been feeling a bit responsible myself," thought Paragrin, and shivered.

"Are you cold?" asked Cam.

"Of course. Aren't you?"

"No, not yet, anyway." He moved closer. "Here, I've got on a heavier jacket. Maybe if I put my arm around you—"

"Stop it!" Paragrin cried, breaking from his hold.

"I'm sorry, I didn't mean anything!" said Cam quickly. "I didn't mean to—"

"Come on, you fellows!" Kerk called, turning back

to stare at them. "This isn't the time for a stroll."

"Coming," said Paragrin, her eyes still fixed on Cam; then she wrapped her jacket tighter and hurried on.

Cam stood alone, his shoulders sagging, then followed the others slowly through the snow.

By noon, the gentle snowfall had turned to a blizzard. The wind rose again and howled through the trees, sending the bitter cold cutting into their skin. The travelers moved on as best they could, but the hopelessness of their situation loomed larger with every painful step, and at last they fell together, huddled in the midst of the storm, to wait for hunger or cold to claim them.

Paragrin looked through frosted lashes to Cam's drawn face and wished then that she hadn't acted so foolishly. She opened her lips to tell him so, but no words came; so she forced her hand from her pocket and pushed it to his. At first he couldn't even feel her touch, but then as the meager warmth came to him, he looked across at her, surprised.

"Oh, Dear Father," said Kerk, staring past them into the snow. "Have I gone mad? Can it possibly be real?"

"What?"

"There's someone out there," he said. "Look!"

Paragrin turned to the wind. "I see it, too!" she cried.

"Hurry! Follow!" shouted Cam, and the three of them rose and stumbled after it, calling out; but the shadow in the snow said nothing. It only moved slowly ahead of them, its cloak blowing about it, silently.

For an hour or two it led them, until the companions found themselves, at last, at the edge of the forest. Staggering forward, they came out from under the trees to stand on the snowy bank of the River Melde.

"Oh, thank the Maker!" Kerk cried.

"I can hardly believe it," said Cam.

"I can," Paragrin said with a laugh. "We're free!"

"Stay where you are," came a voice, and the travelers spun around to find themselves confronted by six warriors with long pointed spears, all of them so bundled in clothes and wooden armor that only their eyes showed through.

"What is this?" said Kerk. "Are we back at the Melde?"

"Far from it," said the voice—it belonged to the largest of the bundles, who poked at Kerk with its spear—"though you'll wish you were, before this day is through. Bodurtha, you and Micolette cover their eyes," it said. "Maradam, Katherette, Norrina, you tend to their wrists."

"I'll not be anyone's prisoner," Kerk shouted, alarmed, and backed away, trying to force his fingers to make a fist.

He was angry, but to her own surprise, Paragrin found she was grateful. If the warriors would only take them out of the snow, she would go any way they liked.

"Kerk, please," said Cam, as his hands, gray with cold, were bound, "we're none of us in any shape to fight."

"We have a stubborn one, I see," said the voice, and laughed. "Very well"—and it threw aside its spear. "Come, little man, try something."

Kerk's eyes flashed, and he rushed toward the warrior, but it grabbed his outstretched arm, and with an abrupt

64

twist flipped him up into the air and down to the ground.

"Dear Essai!" whispered Cam.

"Enough?" said the bundle, retrieving its weapon.

Kerk lay there for a moment stunned, then rose, furious, to fight again. This time, though, the warrior swung back its spear and brought it down on his head.

Cam cried out, but Paragrin was too dull to react. Another blast of wind broke against her, and she sank into the snow.

At the Colony, Ram padded back and forth in front of the fire, muttering, his fingers twisting anxiously around themselves. He started when a sudden gush of cold air blew across the floor, and he looked up to see his son.

The conqueror had returned, his huge ungraceful form bent and beaten, his brawny arms hanging impotent at his sides. About his shoulders, where his brazen cape had been, a mantle of snow rode instead, thick and melting now around his neck. His hair was frozen, his boots caked with ice, and as he looked out from a grim, unyielding face, his dark eyes spoke all there was to say.

But the old man didn't listen.

"No!" he said, running toward him. "You can't turn back now. You can't have failed *again*!" he cried.

And Trag raised up his heavy hand and struck him.

PART TWO

11

"Gret! Oh, Gret, *wake up!*"

Paragrin heard those words from somewhere outside the warm haziness of her body. She heard, but couldn't answer; opening her eyes, her mouth, to the outer world seemed too much of a labor, so she lay there, mute and complaisant, until all at once a fine tingling sensation spread through her limbs. It gave her strength and the desire, suddenly, to be freed from her privacy. With a gasp, she broke through; her eyes opened, and she saw Cam bending over her.

"It worked!" he exclaimed. "Gret, are you all right? We were so worried!"

"I think I'm all right," said Paragrin. "What happened?"

"It would seem," came a voice, "that you stayed too long in the cold."

Paragrin turned and saw a woman kneeling at her side. The stranger had a slight form, fine gold hair faded white at the crown, and a directness in her eyes that seemed to demand the answers to seven questions at once. Paragrin sat up quickly, unable to look away from the woman's searching gaze. "Have—have I done something wrong?" she asked, in a small voice.

The woman's eyes widened, then she laughed. "Of course not; it's my fault for not coming to you sooner," she said.

Paragrin stared at her.

"Sometimes I forget," said the woman, "how delicate people are."

"Then it was *you* in the snow!" Paragrin exclaimed. "You brought us out of the woods!"

"And into a prison," added another voice. Kerk was sitting a little way off, frowning, and Paragrin looked from him to the room they were in. It was an odd, rocky sort of chamber, with two torches set into the walls, and a doorway—she suddenly realized—that was blocked by a sturdy wooden gate.

"I see it differently," said the woman as Paragrin looked back at her suspiciously. "But enough; I am Jentessa, the Holy Intermediator of the Ductae."

"The—the Holy what?" Cam faltered.

"The Holy Intermediator," she replied, "the person selected to act as a medium between the Maker and the people."

"Oh," he said. "Well, I'm Cam, and my brother there, is Kerk. We're . . . normal people."

"That we will see," said Jentessa. "And you?" she asked, turning to Paragrin.

70

The eyes were searching her again, and Paragrin moved her gaze. "Gret," she said, glancing defiantly at Cam; "it's *Gret*."

"I *told* her it was Gret," he returned, defensive.

"Of course you did," said the woman, and rose from Paragrin's side. "I must have forgotten."

"Why are you keeping us?" Kerk demanded. "Where are we, really? What happened to those men that met us at the riverbank?"

Jentessa smiled. "Here's one of them now," she said. "Bodurtha, it's time for me to go." And a warrior, armed with a spear, appeared from behind the gate.

All three of the companions stared, for Bodurtha wasn't a man at all, but a firm young woman dressed in trousers and a coarse-looking jerkin.

"It can't be," Kerk exclaimed. "*She* didn't fight me."

"You're right," said Jentessa, as the woman let her out. "That was Atanelle, the head of our small band of warriors." The gate was closed again with a commanding thud.

"But please, why are we prisoners?" asked Paragrin, rising to her feet.

Jentessa paused and, reaching back through the bars, laid her warm hand on Paragrin's cheek. The fine tingle that she had felt before came to Paragrin again, and she looked at the woman, puzzled. "It is only for a short time, I promise you," said Jentessa softly.

"Can't you let us free?" asked Cam.

"That is not in my power, but in my leader's."

"You're not the leader?"

"Of course not," Jentessa said with a laugh. "Now

71

you must all be patient for a little while longer. Food will be brought for you soon, and I will see you get mats and blankets, although I think you'll find the temperature of our cave quite pleasant after another hour or so. And then, when you're feeling stronger tomorrow, you'll be taken before our leader."

"But who is your—" Cam began.

Jentessa shook her head. "Not now," she said, and disappeared with the warrior down the passageway.

The companions looked at one another helplessly.

"Did she say 'cave'?" asked Paragrin, after a moment.

"Can you believe it?" Kerk cried.

"It's true," said Cam, "though I don't know where, or really how we got here. It seemed we walked a long way—you were carried—but they had Kerk and me blindfolded the whole time, and we were feeling too faint to pay close attention anyhow."

"I was unconscious for the start of the trip," said Kerk. "Atanelle, that head warrior, hit me with his spear."

"I saw," said Paragrin.

"But this is the real surprise," said Cam, "we didn't just walk; toward the end of the journey we were all of us put on a raft and pushed across the River to the other side!"

Paragrin stared at him. "Over the water? But no one's ever crossed the River!"

"So we thought," said Cam, "yet it would seem these people have been doing it all along."

"Who can they be?" she said. "They don't look Meldish. They're unlike any I've ever seen."

"Did you see the way Kerk was flipped into the air?"

Cam exclaimed. "It was amazing. I've never known such a way to fight."

"Well, I'll tell you this," said Kerk, "we're not going to be prisoners long. All we've got to do is see this Ruler. I'll be able to talk our way out of this somehow, you'll see."

The other two looked doubtful, but Kerk, feeling better, settled himself back to await the arrival of food.

Jentessa was as good as her word, and within the hour, they had eaten and fallen to a well-deserved sleep—all except for Paragrin, who stayed awake a little longer, staring into the torches' flames, and thinking. To her own surprise, she found she wasn't even worried about what would happen to them; somehow, the look in Jentessa's eyes had reassured her, convinced her that the caves weren't at all as malevolent as Kerk thought. She sighed, and her gaze lit on Cam, lying beside her on his mat.

"You didn't tell her the truth, did you?" she thought, and after a moment, reached out and laid her fingers gently against his face. He stirred suddenly in his sleep, and Paragrin jumped, snatching her hand back again; but Cam only sighed and was still.

She breathed easier then and, pulling her blanket around her, lay down on her own mat and allowed her eyes to close. The traumas of the Melde, of the storm, fell away from her, and she slept better that night than she had in a long, long time.

12

"It's time to rise."

The companions woke to find Jentessa standing over them, a tray full of steaming bowls in her hands. Paragrin sat up drowsily, savoring the smell of the hot cereal, and thought for a moment that she was back at Lexterre, until she saw the gate again—and Bodurtha with a spear behind it.

"Is it morning?" she asked.

"Well into it," said Jentessa, passing a bowl to each of them. "The sun is out for the first time in days, although, of course, you can't tell that from here. Days, nights . . . it makes little difference in a cave."

"Where did you get this?" Cam asked, tasting the cooked wheat. "It's delicious."

"There are fields—almost as rich as the Melde's—hidden behind the mountain. Now eat quickly, you have only a few minutes before Atanelle comes to take you to see our leader."

"Atanelle . . ." muttered Kerk. "Finally I get to meet him again."

"Jentessa, where do your people come from?" asked Cam. "I never knew other folk existed, apart from the Colonists."

The woman smiled. "We *are* Colonists," she said, "or used to be."

"You lived in the Melde?" he exclaimed.

"All of us have our roots in the Colony; that is where Essai chose to have Its people live."

"*Its* people?" said Paragrin. "You mean *His*, don't you?"

Jentessa stared at her. "I do not," she returned, and stood up so abruptly with her tray that Paragrin looked back, surprised. "Almost forty years ago my leader predicted this would happen," she said, shaking her head. "I did not believe her Partner capable of such a lie, yet he was—and passed it down to his son, and to his son's son, and now . . . even you believe it."

"*Her* Partner?" Kerk said with a frown. "What do you mean—your leader's not a man?"

Heavy footsteps sounded in the tunnel. Jentessa turned to listen, and the companions, exchanging looks, got to their feet uneasily. The noise grew louder, more menacing, and suddenly the rest of the warriors appeared before the gate, heavily armed with blades and spears. The chief stood in front, splendid in a broad green belt, and smiled darkly at the prisoners.

75

"In answer to your question," said Jentessa, turning back to the astonished companions, "there hasn't been a man among us for thirty-seven years."

"Oh, my Father," breathed Kerk.

Atanelle laughed. "You look horrified," she said, unlocking the gate. "You men think so highly of yourselves"—and she poked at Paragrin with her spear. "Go on, all of you, turn about and put your hands behind your backs."

Paragrin stayed as she was, gaping. Never had she seen such a woman before. Woman!—the chief didn't look much older than *she* was, but her arms were firm and muscled, and she had a solid square head that rose forcefully from her broad shoulders. She wore heavy trousers and boots, as Paragrin did, but made no attempt to hide the natural curves of her body; and her hair, instead of being cropped, was long and woven into a fat braid that hung down her back.

"What are you staring at?" Atanelle demanded, and pushed Paragrin around to the wall. "Hurry now, Maradam, Micolette, put on the ropes; and you, Katherette, get the blinds."

"There'll be no need for blinds," said Jentessa.

"But you know men aren't supposed to see—" the warrior began.

"No blinds," said Jentessa.

"Well . . . no blinds, then," said Atanelle after a moment. "Just make those ropes all the more secure."

"It was you who flipped me into the snow?" Kerk said, appalled.

"That was just a warning," returned the chief, and

she pulled the three bound companions into a row. "If you make any more trouble, little man, you'll see what I'm really capable of"—she dared him with a smile. "Now walk," she barked, and everyone walked.

On through the rocky maze of tunnels and chambers they went, and Paragrin could hardly take in what she saw. There were rooms in the cave; not naked holes like the prison, but real rooms, with tables and beds and tapestries on the walls, rugs on the floors, and pillowed chairs. Why, it was practically cheerful.

And then they passed into a larger chamber, where a whole crowd of people had gathered. They were all women, as Jentessa had said, but Paragrin had never seen women like these. They weren't like villagers, for their hair was uncovered, but they didn't look like Colonists either. These women, even the older ones, were strong and healthy, and their clothing, though simple, was of a distinctly handsome weave. They seemed altogether a proud assemblage, and their eyes, glistening in the brightness of the torches, returned with equal intensity the curious stares they received.

"Men," Paragrin realized, "must be rare sights indeed"; and suddenly she felt very out of place.

The warriors led them out of the chamber and down a long, winding tunnel, until at last they stopped at the entrance to a room. How large or splendid it was Paragrin couldn't see, for unlike the bright rooms they had passed, this one was only dimly lit. At first she thought that there must have been some mistake; surely a leader wouldn't stay in such murky surroundings as this—even in Lexterre, her brother had the best house in the village—but Atanelle whispered to all of them, prisoners and warriors alike, to look sharp; and squaring her shoulders, she marched them into the room.

13

There was definitely a presence in the large stone chair that jutted out from the cavern wall, but the sparse lighting was so ineffective that Paragrin had to strain her eyes to make out the form. Gradually, as her eyes adjusted to the darkness, she saw a woman, solemn and stony, sunk down in the crude throne, her arms out in front of her, hands grasping the sides of the chair, and her feet planted firmly on the ground. Her hair was black and wavy, like Paragrin's; but the girl could see even in the dimness that it was streaked with gray. She wore no elaborate costume, just a black skirt that reached to her calves, and a simple jacket held in at the waist by a belt. The only thing that suggested her lofty position was a light-colored cape draped over her breastbone, which hung, motionless, across the arm of the throne.

Paragrin stared in wonder and was startled to realize that although the woman had not spoken a word since they entered, she was staring back at them. Unlike the women in the other chamber, though, her look was not one of fascination, but of dulled disgust.

The woman stirred finally and turned her head to the right, where Jentessa was standing.

"These travelers are from Lexterre, my leader," Jentessa began; "a town that broke from the Colony ten years ago, and that is governed by a man named Strap."

"Who is this Strap?" demanded the woman.

"Trag's son," said Jentessa, and the woman gave a bitter laugh.

"I might have known," she muttered.

The Holy Intermediator continued, motioning toward the prisoners. "This first young man is called Kerk," she said.

Kerk looked back at the throne, dumbfounded.

"This other young man is Cam," said Jentessa. "The two of them are brothers." Cam blanched as the Ruler moved her leaden gaze to him, but she made no comment, and nodded for Jentessa to finish.

"And this last young person is called . . ." Jentessa smiled. "I've forgotten your name again," she said.

"Gret," Paragrin answered, her voice high and uncertain.

"Of course. Gret. And my leader," she announced to the companions, "is Zessiper, chosen by the Maker to rule."

"Chosen to rot in a hole, rather," Zessiper returned.

She sat up slowly in her chair, her gray eyes illuminated then by the torchlight. "Sitting here all these years, like a child playing at miracles, hoping that someday, something would finally—"

"Your plans for the prisoners—" Jentessa interrupted, "what are they?"

The leader scowled and sank back into her chair, her eyes disappearing again in the shadows. "What do I care?" she said, waving her hand in irritation. "Do as you like with them."

Jentessa looked to the warrior chief. "Take them back to their room then," she said. "I'll follow shortly." She smiled reassuringly at Paragrin, and then the girl, along with her fellow prisoners, was led out of the dim chamber, and back through the winding tunnels to the cell.

"What sort of an upside-down place is this?" Kerk snorted when they were left alone again.

Paragrin leaned up against the gate and tried to sort her thoughts. She knew now that a woman warrior had been only the first of her surprises. Zessiper was frightening and strange, brooding alone in the dark, as if she carried some great sorrow on her shoulders; and yet Paragrin couldn't deny the fascination she felt for her. Zessiper seemed so much like a ruler—so obviously in power. For a woman's word to be called for and respected—well, it was something Paragrin had only imagined. Strange or not, it was admirable. She turned to share her thoughts with the brothers, but stopped, wondering if they would understand.

When Jentessa came back to them, she and Cam exploded with questions, but the Intermediator only shook her head. "The time will come for you to learn the answers," she said, "but first steps must come first. Now, as you have heard, you are in my charge."

"And you're going to release us?" said Kerk.

"That is not among the choices Zessiper gave me," Jentessa said with a smile.

He frowned. "It's not, is it? Well, why don't you tell her that—"

"Trust me."

"I trusted you in the snow, and look what's happened!"

"Kerk!" Cam chided.

"No, he is right to distrust," said Jentessa, "if he puts his faith in nothing but himself. I'm sorry I cannot convince you of my sincerity, Kerk, yet I'm afraid you have no choice but to follow the steps laid out for you."

"What steps?" asked Cam. "Where are they going to lead us?"

"To something very important and very necessary— not only to you, but to all the far-flung children of the Colony."

"And we have a part to play in this?" asked Paragrin.

Jentessa nodded. "Yet here I am answering questions that I said must wait. Enough. Come, child," she said, holding out her hand to Paragrin, "it all begins with you."

"Me?" she asked, astonished. The boys stared at her.

"Yes. You will leave the prison for the remainder of your stay."

"What about my friends?" she said, taking her hand.

"Yes, what about his friends?" demanded Kerk.

"In time, I am sure that you, too, will be released." Jentessa led Paragrin firmly from the cell.

"In time? What time?" Kerk cried. He jumped up to try to stop Bodurtha from locking the gate, but was too late. "Let me out of here!" he bellowed, shaking the bars.

"Kerk, calm down," Cam pleaded.

"Little Gret, come back!" he wailed, but Paragrin, her fingers tightening around her hidden iron, followed Jentessa and the warrior down the passage, until the prison with its captives was far from her sight.

14

"This is where you'll sleep and take your meals," Jentessa said when she had led Paragrin away from the main cluster of chambers to her room. It was smaller than the prison yet much more comfortable, with a bed, a thickly woven rug, and, the girl was surprised to see, an unbarred entrance. "You understand," the woman continued, "why you cannot stay with the rest of us. Zessiper would not approve."

"I understand that," Paragrin said quietly, "but I don't understand why you gave me freedom, and didn't give it to my friends."

"Don't you?" said the woman, and gazed upon her with the same intensity as she had when they first met. "You have something to learn about yourself," she said at last.

"What is it?" Paragrin returned, defensive.

Jentessa smiled. "Just listen, watch, and think," she said, "because the state of the Colony, of Lexterre, and even of the cave have shown you nothing that is natural, nothing that is as Essai meant for it to be. But here at least there exists that part of Its plan that you have never seen, never known to be possible, although you have felt it in your soul. It is an essential part, and you must come to know and cherish it, or all else is useless."

Paragrin looked at her. "What is this part?" she asked.

"You may wander through the chambers and passages as you will," said Jentessa, "but do not leave them. Nor should you visit your friends for now; concentrate on the women instead." She moved out into the tunnel. "Remember that I will be here for you always, only come and find me if you have a question."

"Wait! How do I—"

"Listen, watch, and think," Jentessa repeated, and disappeared.

Paragrin frowned, and sat, confused, on the bed. What was it she was supposed to think about? What could she possibly learn from this peculiar civilization? Pensive, she reached up to tuck a loose tress beneath her cap— but caught herself. She paused, surprised. It had been a long time since she had forgotten she'd cut her hair.

There was a metal mirror set into the wall of her room, and Paragrin rose from the bed to see herself. She hadn't examined her image since that fateful night in Lexterre, and now she stood and compared. She was leaner perhaps, her hair a little wilder, and Strap's clothes certainly the worse for the wear; but they still hung

85

on her loosely, and the boyish look she had made for herself remained. Paragrin studied the lumpish jacket and frowned; then, gathering the extra material behind her, she turned to inspect the curve of her waist, when suddenly Ellagette and Aridda seemed to flash beside her in the reflection, their lips wide in mocking laughter.

She gasped, and looked again. They were gone, but Paragrin's heart beat with such awful vehemence that after she shoved the mirror under the bed, she pulled her jacket out again and tousled her hair before leaving to look for the women.

The Ductae were courteous enough when she walked among them that morning, but the girl suspected it was all due to some order of Jentessa's. They stared at her so, when they thought she wasn't looking, and she felt their hostility; so after a few hours Paragrin abandoned them and set out instead to explore the cave.

She learned in that afternoon that it was not nearly so large or confusing as she had first thought. Once she had grown accustomed to the irregular levels and spaces, she could travel it all with ease, or at least anywhere the torchlight permitted. There was, of course, one exception; Zessiper's dim room, far away from any of the others, was understood to be inaccessible to everyone, unless Zessiper herself said otherwise.

The leader spent most of her time, the girl noticed, in her private darkness. When she had been among her people that day, she had rarely smiled, and then only when Jentessa had been with her. Judging from her first sight of them together, Paragrin had supposed that the two older women didn't like each other, but she wondered, later, if that thought had been wrong. It was only through Jentessa's tireless efforts that Zessiper smiled at all, or stirred from her room. The woman with the healing hands seemed to have the same sort of comforting effect on her that she had had on Paragrin, and the girl was glad Zessiper had someone to share her sorrow with. There were many times that day when she wanted to go and talk to the leader herself—or at least sit and watch her—but Zessiper encouraged no conversation, and indeed, Paragrin's presence seemed to offend her.

When Paragrin asked Jentessa why this was so, the woman explained that Zessiper had had terrible experiences with men long ago, and had blamed and hated the whole sex for the sins of a few.

"But doesn't she realize how wrong that is?"

Jentessa shook her head. "She does not; for the few hurt her so deeply that she is blinded by pain."

"What did they do?" Paragrin asked in a whisper.

"One took her city," the woman replied, "and wounded her pride; but the other took her daughter and with that, her heart."

After another day had passed, and Paragrin's curiosity about the cave had been well satisfied, she turned once more to the Ductae. They seemed now to be used to her, and she to them, and although Paragrin still didn't join in any of the functions they performed, she watched intently and listened in on their evening meetings.

Their life together was not at all what she had expected; she didn't quite know *what* she had expected, something more like the way the girls at Lexterre acted around each other at the Maiden Dances, perhaps: competitive, and not very cordial. Paragrin couldn't remember ever making friends with another girl, and the comradery she saw between the women came as a great surprise to her. There were incivilities between some, of course, but when they did come to blows, it was due to some difference of opinion, not rivalry of beauty or domestic achievement, and Paragrin found this much more agreeable. They talked together and laughed just as she had seen men do in Lexterre, and yet, somehow, they never seemed to surrender their femininity in doing it. Here the entire question of what was "feminine," and what was not, never arose. The women did everything—they hunted and fished and farmed—they even protected the cave with spears and knives—and no one ever rushed out to bring them all back inside, telling them that such things were forbidden. And most amazing of all to Paragrin—on top of everything else—these women even knew how to cook. And some of them *liked* it.

And so, when Paragrin returned from the bustle of the central chamber to her room, she lingered in the doorway, her fingers twisting around themselves, and stared at the mirror beneath her bed. On an impulse, she snatched it from the floor and set it again into the wall, standing back and daring it to frighten her. Yet no other images shone forth but her own, and as she relaxed her gaze, she saw in her reflection a young woman who looked . . . all right.

She smiled and thought how ridiculous she looked in her brother's oversized clothes. Reaching up underneath the jacket, she unwound the strip of blanket that had bound her and, with a grateful sigh, dropped it to the floor.

"Well, my young friend," came a voice, and Paragrin spun about to find Jentessa standing in the doorway. "Welcome back."

15

Paragrin glanced at her, embarrassed. "I was just playing a game," she said.

"Of course," returned Jentessa, "and a helpful one at times, wasn't it?"

"I suppose," the girl replied, "but I don't want to play it anymore."

Jentessa smiled. "Well, Gret, you'll have to be reintroduced to Zessiper now that you're not a man."

"My name, it's—it's not Gret," she faltered.

"No?"

"No, that was just part of the game. I'm called Paragrin."

"Ah, a lovely name—and the young men, too, will have to be told."

"Oh!" Paragrin's face fell. "Kerk is never going to understand this."

"He must be told, nonetheless," said Jentessa, and sat down on the bed. "How do you think Cam will react?"

Paragrin looked away. "Oh, he knows. He's known for a long time, I guess. He must think I'm awfully foolish."

"Has he ever said so? Has he ever mocked you in any way?"

"Well, no. In fact, through it all, he's been . . ."

"Been what?" asked the woman.

Paragrin shook her head. "Nothing. Can I have some different clothes now? These have never really fit."

"Yes, there's a stack of extra clothing in the storage chamber. Come with me, and we'll see if we can find— is there something wrong?"

"I think I had better go myself," Paragrin said quietly, remembering the hidden iron. She trusted Jentessa, and yet somehow she didn't feel it was time. Tempira had said there would be a time. She looked down at her boots, avoiding what she assumed was Jentessa's curious gaze.

But the Holy Intermediator only smiled. "After you've changed and visited your friends," she said, "how would you like to join the rest of us for dinner?"

"Oh, I would!"

"Very well, I'll see you then," Jentessa said, moving out into the passageway. "Good luck with Kerk," she added and went away.

When Paragrin was sure Jentessa had gone, she left the chamber and made her way to the storage room. Luckily no one else was there, and kneeling by the pile of clothes, she unfolded and refolded the worn material until she found a wide black skirt. She liked it immediately because it reminded her of Zessiper, and finally discarding her brother's trousers, she pulled the skirt over her head and down to her waist, where it settled comfortably on her hips.

A good blouse was harder to find because it had to be full enough to hide the Amulet, but eventually she found one that was suitable, and looking to the entrance to make certain no one was watching, she flung off the jacket and pulled on the blouse, tucking the iron beneath it. The boots she kept, for despite their ill fit, she had grown attached to them, and they were nicer than any she had seen the Ductae wear.

Once she had finished with her dressing, she stood in the middle of the chamber and surveyed herself. To her delight, the Ductae skirt was wonderfully unconfining—better than pants, even—and she twirled, making the skirt fan out around her. It was very satisfying.

As she walked back through the passageway to her room, Paragrin came to the bend in the tunnel that led to the prison. She stopped and remembered: the boys. Her resolution faltered, but Jentessa's trust in her forbade any escape, so she turned reluctantly into the passage.

As she moved down toward the prison, she hoped against odds that Kerk would be fast asleep in the middle of the afternoon; and as she drew closer, she saw to her great surprise that he actually *was* asleep, curled up on his mat. Cam was awake, sitting with his back against the gate, and she went forward, heartened.

"Cam!"

He turned—and his mouth fell open. "Paragrin!" he exclaimed, and scrambled to his feet, practically bursting through the gate with the strength of his greeting.

She blushed. "Well, it's not a secret anymore," she said.

He nodded. "I'm glad!"

Then there came an awkward silence, with each of them glancing at the other one, uncertain, until Cam finally said, "You're looking well, Paragrin; very well."

"Oh, thank you. You're looking . . ." She paused.

"Not so well?" Cam said with a rueful smile.

"I'm sorry you've had to be shut up in here," Paragrin said. "It's terrible, I know."

"It's not been so bad for me," Cam returned, "but for Kerk, it *has* been terrible. You know how much energy he usually has. These couple of days with nothing to do but sit have been very hard. I've tried to reason with him, telling him that it's only for a little time, but he won't listen to me anymore. I don't blame him. I can't give any promises."

Paragrin's hands tightened around the bars. "Why is he asleep?" she asked. "It's daytime still."

"He's slept a lot today. I don't think he's well. He hasn't even touched his last two meals! Paragrin, do you have any power now that you're one of them? Can you get us out?"

"I don't know. I'm not really one of them yet. I just revealed myself to Jentessa, as it is."

"Oh . . ."

"But don't worry, I'll get you free somehow. Jentessa's

93

going to get me in to see Zessiper again, now that I'm not a man. I'll convince her to let you go. I'll—"

"Oh, rot . . ." muttered Kerk.

Paragrin's eyes widened, and she froze, bracing herself for anything. Kerk rolled over onto his back; and when he saw her, he got slowly to his feet, coming to peer at her through the bars. He did look sick, Paragrin thought; pale and unsteady.

"What are you wearing a skirt for, Little Gret?" he demanded.

Cam and Paragrin exchanged glances. "Well, you see, Kerk," said Cam, "Gret's really a girl."

"A what?"

"I'm Paragrin," she said. "Remember? From Lexterre."

Kerk stared at her.

"I—I dressed up like a boy and cut my hair and everything because I was banished," she explained hastily, "and thought it would be better—easier—if I looked different, and when you ran into me, I didn't see any reason to change, because then you might have sent me back or something, so I said my name was Gret, and . . . you believed me."

"Paragrin? From Lexterre?"

"Yes."

"You're a girl!" he cried, twisting his face into what Paragrin translated as rage; even Cam backed against the gate.

"Yes!" she whispered.

Then Kerk let loose and laughed harder than he had ever laughed before. Cam broke into a smile; so did

94

Paragrin, who was so relieved she didn't know quite what to do.

"I thought you'd be angry," she said.

"Angry?" Kerk exclaimed. "Great Maker, that's the funniest thing I ever heard. And I believed you all along. You believed it too, didn't you, Partner?"

"Well, actually, I—"

"I did think you were a little weird," Kerk continued, "going into the woods all the time, and never swimming in the—oho!" he cried again. "You got quite a show, didn't you, girl?" and this brought on a whole new peal of laughter.

Cam reddened.

"Well, I'm glad you're not angry," she said, reassured to see the old Kerk at last.

But his humor slipped away as the joke subsided, and he pressed himself against the gate. "Can you get me out of here, Paragrin?" he entreated.

She sobered too, her heart aching to see him so strange again. "Yes, I'll try. I will! I promise."

"Soon?"

"Yes, I promise."

"Good," he said. "That's good." He sank back down on his mat. "I don't know why I'm so tired," he said, and closed his eyes.

Paragrin winced.

"I'll take care of him," said Cam. "You go talk to Zessiper."

She nodded, and turned to go.

"Paragrin?" Cam whispered.

She turned back. "Yes?"

"What did you mean when you said you were banished? Did Strap tell you to leave?"

"Yes."

"Whatever for?"

Paragrin bit her lip. "For not being enough of a woman, I suppose," she said.

"Oh, Paragrin!" Cam stretched his arm through the gate.

She pulled back; his reach faltered. Then she looked into his eyes and, without quite knowing why she did it, offered back her hand.

He pressed it in his own, gently. "Strap was wrong," he said, and went to care for his brother.

Paragrin looked down at the two of them in silence; then she turned and ran as fast as she could through the tunnel, her eyes brimming with tears.

16

"Jentessa!" Paragrin cried, bursting into her room, "I
need to—" She stopped, blinking; Jentessa wasn't to
be found, but there, shooting across the floor, was a
brilliant shaft of light. It came from an opening she had
never seen before in the side of the chamber. She wondered at it, and at the great slab of stone that rested
now against the wall. "Jentessa?" she said again, and
cautiously approaching the gap in the rock, she stepped
through into the glare—and caught her breath.

"Sweet Divine," she whispered.

Revealed before her was a magnificent towering chamber, its stony sides stretching in abrupt and dizzying
angles to the very crest of the mountain. The room was
bathed in shimmering daylight, for unlike any of the
other chambers, the rock at its summit was parted, and

the rays of the sun spilled into its chasm. And down at the bottom, a little apart from where Paragrin stood, was a pool of clear water cradled in the rock itself, which captured in its glittering surface the blue of the sky above.

"Sweet Divine," she said again.

"Precisely."

Paragrin turned to see Jentessa standing beside her. "What is this place?" she breathed. "It's lovely."

"It is the sacred chamber. Reaching from the sky down to the depths of the earth, it encompasses Essai's creation. It is a room I use for meditation."

"Oh; then I'm sorry to have to disturb you, Jentessa, but I need to get in to see Zessiper. Now!"

"Why? Has something happened?"

"It's Kerk. He's so miserable. And poor Cam! I can't have them stay in that awful prison anymore, not while I'm free. I promised I'd get them out, and she's the only one who can do it, isn't she? You said you couldn't."

"No, I cannot."

"Then reintroduce me now, please! Or I'll go in and see her myself, I swear I will."

Jentessa stared at her. "I did not think this meeting would happen so soon," she said.

"Jentessa, *please*!"

The woman studied her for a moment longer, then moved her gaze away. "Very well."

Paragrin smiled, and started back into the bedroom, but Jentessa put out a hand. "No, I will go first and prepare her. Stay here until I return"—and stepping through into her room, Jentessa disappeared.

It seemed like hours that she was gone. Paragrin grew impatient and paced the chamber, gazing up at the distant patch of sky, and then at the jagged walls of stone that climbed up to it. There was something about the magnificence of the room that made her feel uneasy. After all, she had denounced the Divine Father; perhaps it was sacrilegious for her to be there at all. She moved her sights to the more humble surroundings of the cavern floor.

After walking around the room for a minute, she came upon a small earthen bowl filled with dye, which was set upon the ground. She had used paint before, when Aridda had forced her to decorate pottery in Lexterre, but it puzzled her as to why Jentessa would do such menial work in her sacred room. Then she saw that the wall to her left had a little picture painted on it; and then she saw not one picture, but many. Stepping back, she knew the first figure was actually the last in a long procession: a parade of people marching two by two, and although simply drawn, they made of themselves a beautifully lyrical design. Paragrin was charmed, and looked closer. Every marching pair was a man and a woman, and each man had a rectangle painted on his chest, and each woman had an oval. This was true for all the figures—except at the end, where she had come across the bowl. There, she realized that the figure she had seen at first was really only half a picture—just a woman, freshly painted, without even an oval to decorate her chest. Paragrin had to fight the urge to take the paint and put one there herself, it looked so naked, but she dared not touch it, and forced herself

99

back to ponder its meaning. She didn't quite know what it was, but there was something familiar about the symbols.

"Paragrin."

She turned; Jentessa was in the doorway.

"Go. It is time."

Forgetting the mural in the instant, she went to her. "Will Zessiper release the boys?" she asked.

"No," Jentessa replied. "You will."

Paragrin looked at her, not understanding, but the woman only took her hand and held it. "When you talk to Zessiper, do not just try to convince her of her wrongs. Listen to her story, my child, *listen*, for it is the crux upon which everything else depends." She paused. "Now go."

Paragrin, after a second's hesitation, went back through the opening to the tunnels.

When she had gone, Jentessa stood for a moment alone. Then, decisively, she swept over to the mural and, delicately dipping her finger into the paint, drew a little oval on the last figure's chest.

"At last," she said, and smiled.

17

"You are apparently determined to talk to me," Zessiper's voice droned from the darkness.

Paragrin strained her eyes, and the woman's face and form emerged slowly from the murkiness. "Yes," she whispered. Zessiper was sunk down in the throne, just as she had been found before.

"I must say that I find you uncommon," the woman continued, turning her hard gray eyes on Paragrin. "Why would you want to disguise yourself as a man? I can't think of anything more distasteful."

"I need to talk to you about my friends," said the girl.

"Oh? I suppose you're going to tell me *they're* women, too?"

Paragrin smiled. "No, they're men, and—and they're miserable."

"Well," Zessiper returned, "I can understand that. If I were a man, I'd be miserable, too."

"Stop it, please. You have to release them!"

Zessiper drew herself up in the throne and leaned forward. "I don't have to *do* anything," she said.

"Why not let them free? They've never done you any harm."

"Never done me any harm?" Zessiper echoed. "Why, if it hadn't been for the treachery and ambition of their sex, we women would never have been forced from the Colony! And they wouldn't even stop at that; they came in numbers to claim or murder us, forcing the few that were left to hide here under the earth, helpless and beaten!" She trembled with anger. "And you dare to say they've never done me harm. They've done every woman harm!"

"But my friends didn't do that," Paragrin insisted, trying not to let her fear of the woman get the better of her. "If you let them go free, they'd return to Lexterre and never come back."

"Oh, stupid girl," Zessiper muttered, "how little you know of men." She paused, watching her, then demanded, "Who rules Lexterre?"

"Strap."

"Yes, Strap; son of Trag, grandson of Ram . . . do you think he'll be content, once he learns of our hidden home, to forget it?"

Paragrin didn't know.

"He won't be!" Zessiper answered. "He'll come, just like his father and his grandfather before him, to take whatever vestige of pride we have left."

102

"But I don't understand. What exactly did they do?"

Zessiper stared at her, incredulous. "Do you mean to say you don't know?"

"I—I just had always assumed that what happened before was like what happens now," said Paragrin. "I was never told any different."

Zessiper narrowed her eyes; then, after a moment's contemplation, demanded, "Were you taught that the Maker had a gender?"

"Well, Jentessa said that—"

"Forget what Jentessa said! What were you *taught*?"

". . . That It was a man."

"Ha!" Zessiper cried, and leaned back in her throne again to study the girl in silence.

"So are all the young women as ignorant as you about their history?" she asked at last.

"Yes . . . at least in Lexterre."

"Then listen to me," the woman urged, leaning forward again, "and when you go back to your side of the River, tell them all what I am about to tell you; that what exists now is a travesty. Jentessa keeps assuring me that there will come a time when the Maker will return it to the way it was, but it has been thirty-seven years, and I am tired of waiting. Perhaps, if you spread the word of the injustices of our past, it will quicken the return. You will do this?"

Paragrin, much impressed, nodded. "If it's the best thing to do," she whispered.

"Judge for yourself," Zessiper returned, "and listen." Her gaze, for the first time during their meeting, drifted away into the darkness. "Once," she said, "the people lived as one in the Colony, with two equal leaders."

"*Two* leaders?"

"Of course, two—a woman and a man of the Ruling Family."

"But there's never been a woman ruling in the Melde," said Paragrin.

"There had *always* been a woman in the Melde!" Zessiper cried, striking the arm of her throne. "My Maker, how could you nót know that? How could you think it was right for a man to rule alone?"

"I—I never thought it was right," Paragrin stammered.

"For centuries, women ruled beside men! Until a time thirty-seven years ago"—she paused—"when *I* came to power."

"You ruled the Colony?" Paragrin exclaimed, looking across to her with even greater admiration than before. "With Ram?"

"For two months, I had that dishonor," said Zessiper, "then he had the gall, the insolence, to say the Maker condemned my right, and that I should 'step down.' But I knew It would never favor Ram over me. Essai," she said, looking hard at Paragrin, "has no such thing as a gender. It never did. That was Ram's fabrication . . . and he wove it well."

"But it changed whole generations!" Paragrin breathed. "Why did he do such a horrible thing?"

"Because he's the perfect model of a man: ambitious and vain. But I wouldn't stand for his treachery, nor would any of the women. We were strong then," she said with a smile, "and powerful. We left the Colony and went to live across the River in the Western Mountains, to force Ram to take back his false accusation."

"But he didn't," said Paragrin.

"No, he didn't; and when I sent two of my women back to discuss terms with him, he had one murdered. But I avenged her . . ." Zessiper's eyes glowed, and reaching up with one lean hand, she pulled her woven shirt from off her shoulder, revealing a hideous scar. "When a troop of them first came uninvited to our settlement," she said, "they tried to kill me; but we were stronger than they were. I killed *them*. My women and I survived, *thrived*, in fact, alone in our separate land; and when the men came again and again to try to break us, we fended them off, and took only enough prisoners to continue our female race. Ah, it was fine, then! Those years were glorious. There were hundreds and hundreds of us. We had a great future, and, most blessed of all— we had an heir. She was the best thing to come from the separation, and the only good thing I've ever gotten from a man."

Paragrin smiled. "Jentessa told me you had a daughter."

"Yes, I had a daughter," Zessiper said, her eyes shining in the darkness. "Better to me than any sister. She was the brightest, the strongest, the most beautiful young woman of all the Ductae, and my time being past, she was made Ruler." Her voice softened, and she whispered, "I gave her the name . . . Tempira."

Paragrin blanched. "*Tempira?*"

"Yes," Zessiper replied, unconscious of the other's change of color, "but then—then Trag!" She spat. "He

105

murdered her!" She sat up, gripping the arms of the throne, the memory vivid again in her mind. "Ram gave him the leadership, and he charged into our town in the midst of a festival when we were unarmed and helpless. There was hardly a fight. He came with his army and surrounded us, demanding we surrender or be killed. I was in the crowd, I *saw* how he looked at Tempira. She was brave, so very brave, and defied him like a true ruler, but he was stronger and . . . I saw it, but I couldn't—I—" Zessiper shot up from her chair. "I broke away! I was going to save her, kill him, *kill him with my bare hands*, but my town—it was being destroyed—my women, too proud to be his slaves, being murdered—my daughter—oh, Essai! I wanted to go to her. . . ." She trembled, her voice fading, her eyes filling with tears. "I wanted to, but I couldn't. I had to be a ruler before a mother. I had to preserve the Ductae, and let that—that *man*—drag her away to be his whore, to die under him!" Zessiper's face darkened again, and she sank back into her throne, exhausted. "What good was it?" she muttered. "For we didn't even know until too late that he had taken our Oval, too."

Paragrin felt, suddenly, very cold. "Oval?" she whispered.

"Yes. A beautiful Oval Amulet made of iron; the symbol of the Maker's blessing upon the woman who wore it; the true badge of leadership. Tempira had it when she was taken, and it fell into Trag's filthy hands. Now he has both Amulets, and it's lost to us forever!"

"But . . . but what if it had *not* fallen into his hands?" Paragrin quavered. "What if Tempira had kept it hidden, buried in the earth? She—she would have given it to her daughter, wouldn't she have?"

Zessiper looked at her. "If she had had a daughter by that—man—yes. But she couldn't have. If she had, that daughter would have claimed her right to rule long ago."

"Not if she had never been told what the Amulet meant!" Paragrin cried.

Zessiper leaned forward, seizing her by the shoulders. "What are you talking about? What do you know? Tell me!"

"I knew Tempira!" said Paragrin. "In her prison at the courtyard, she was always watching me, but I never knew why; and then one day she beckoned to me, and she was very insistent, and—"

"What did she do?" Zessiper demanded, her eyes wide. "What did she say?"

"She said there would be a time when I could tell, and Dear Essai, I think it's finally come!" Paragrin brought the Amulet out from underneath her blouse. "She called me her daughter, and she gave me *this*."

"Great Maker!" gasped Zessiper. She stared at the Amulet, too stunned to move. Then, carefully, almost fearfully, she reached out with her hand to feel it. Ah! The old iron felt so familiar beneath her fingers. Its texture, its every bump—she knew it. She knew it. Slowly, she raised her eyes and gazed at Paragrin, any trace of anger or condescension gone, and in its place— wonder. "Great Maker," she said again, but this time her voice was soft, and the words were more of a thanks than an exclamation. She lifted her worn brown hands

107

and laid them against Paragrin's face. Gently, she turned the girl's head, her eyes dimming as she tried to match it to another girl's. When she suddenly saw the resemblance, she gasped again, and moving her hands to her own face, muffled the sobs that now came uncontrollably from deep within her tired frame.

Paragrin stood perfectly still. She felt herself unable to move. In one instant, her entire life had changed. With difficulty, she tried to understand who and what it was she had so suddenly become—no longer an outcast, but someone special—someone important—someone whose coming brought tears to the powerful woman before her. The oval in the mural—of course—the Amulet; and the lone woman figure must be . . . herself.

In raising her eyes to Zessiper, Paragrin knew she wasn't the only one who had changed; surely this weeping woman wasn't the same brooding creature she had met before. That had been a stranger; this woman . . . was her grandmother.

As if the thought of their newfound relationship had struck them both at the same time, Zessiper raised her wet eyes from behind her palms and met her gaze. They stared, newly amazed at one another, and trembled in silence, apart. Then Zessiper stretched out her arms and clasped Paragrin fiercely to her bosom.

Grandmother and granddaughter, old Ruler and new, held each other, and their emotions flowed furiously between them; they were as one. And then, after a time, Zessiper released her embrace and held the young woman out from her. Her eyes were red and her voice husky as she said, "I don't even know your name.

Jentessa may have told me, but that was so long ago, I no longer remember."

"It's Paragrin," the girl answered, her voice equally unsteady.

"Par-a-grin," Zessiper repeated, drawing out the sounds. "I won't forget again." She gazed at her dreamily; then, with her face suddenly brightened, she leaped from her chair and took her granddaughter's hand. "Come!" she said, striding to the passageway. "I've kept this miracle to myself long enough. Everyone must be told! Great Maker! Great Maker, we've hope again. *Jentessa!*" she cried, and ran from the room.

18

What took place in the next few hours was a blur to Paragrin; it was all she could do to remember why these strange and remarkable things were happening.

First, Jentessa was found and told. Paragrin remembered that she had smiled a great deal, and had said some words to her—but what they were, she hadn't the faintest idea. And then suddenly everyone knew, and she was brought by Zessiper into the central chamber where all sixty of the Ductae crowded around her, their faces filled with astonishment and awe. Names rushed past as she was reintroduced: Elizanne, Jillian, Janera, Natabarre . . . she could retain none of them. Some of the older women cried, and said how much she looked like her grandmother.

And then the Amulet was brought forth and given

to the crowd. The women had all seen it before, but some only in their infancy, and it was slowly borne from one to the next with great wonder and respect. Zessiper's eyes were never off it, and when at last everybody had had her turn, she took the iron back again, clutched to her breast.

"This is your true leader!" she proclaimed, her lean arm wrapped tightly about Paragrin's waist; and all the Ductae stepped back and bowed their heads in silent veneration. This was astounding enough for the girl, but when Jentessa, Zessiper, and even a dumbstruck Atanelle did the same, she wondered for a moment if she had lost her mind.

Zessiper stepped forward and announced then that a grand ceremony would be held immediately in the new leader's honor. "The largest we can afford!" she exclaimed. "With the most succulent food prepared, and this blessed cave decorated with as much show as such a ceremony deserves. Jentessa!" she said. "It must be held in the sacred chamber."

"Of course, my leader."

"There will my granddaughter Paragrin accept the Oval Amulet officially, and become the right Ruler of the Melde. Now go. Begin the preparations!" she cried. "Great Maker, it's going to happen at last."

And so it was done. The warriors, once again under Atanelle's direction, set forth from the cave to search for barberries, pine cones, and any other natural decorations the season allowed. They brought them back in armfuls, filling the chambers with color and a delicious natural smell.

The fragrance made its way through the tunnels to the ovens, where the other women were busily working. Meats were being cooked, breads were baking, puddings—such as the cave had never known—were bubbling. It was marvelous. It was a time for celebration.

In Zessiper's own room, newly brightened by additional torches, Paragrin herself was being readied. The ill-fitting blouse was replaced, and her grandmother's light-colored cape was draped majestically across her shoulders. Her hair was brushed and pampered, and a coronet of grapevines was woven gracefully through its short locks. Paragrin stood passively, breathlessly, her cheeks flushed with pride and bewilderment.

Zessiper stood near her, cradling the long-lost Amulet again in her hands. Jentessa was there as well, her eyes sparkling as she watched Paragrin's transformation. Then, at a thought, she looked to Zessiper and said, "It is your wish that everyone attend the ceremony, my leader?"

"Of course!" Zessiper returned. "Why do you even ask?"

"A foolish question," Jentessa admitted, and she quickly disappeared down the passageway.

It was time, and the women, their preparations completed, gathered together under the night in the sacred chamber. The torches, set into the stone, burned brightly and cast grand shadows that reached all the way up to the crest and made the surface of the pool glitter like the stars above it. Several of the women brought and played the instruments they had mastered—flutes,

112

drums, and lutes—and filled the cavernous space with strong and stirring music, strange melodies and beautiful; and when Jentessa, fulfilling her role as Holy Intermediator, led Paragrin and Zessiper into the shrine, she chanted in a low, rhythmic voice the words from a time before, as the music swelled beneath her:

"Laudais lu chemnee garai,
   Essai, fee dem tran cetus."

Paragrin walked slowly at Zessiper's side, mesmerized by the haunting music and lights. She followed Jentessa to the very edge of the pool and when she and her grandmother knelt upon the stone, Paragrin gazed up at the Holy Intermediator, filled with a great sense of the woman's wisdom and of her own good fortune—that, with all her turnings in life, she had come at last upon these people.

Jentessa, solemnly dressed in a dark-colored cloak, opened a wooden box that she had carried from her room and, taking from it a handful of sandy earth, sprinkled it over the two of them, saying:

"The Earth envelops and stays the body,
   But the spirit, everlasting, returns;
   Back to the Center, back to the Maker,
   Back to Essai, united, forever."

She motioned the leaders again to stand.

Paragrin got to her feet a little unsteadily and glanced across to the proud figure of her grandmother. How fine she looked! How powerful. The Amulet once more lay against her chest and Paragrin thought how well it looked; how well on *her*, and how ridiculous on her own callow form. Doubt crept over her; how could she ever be the ruler Zessiper was? She felt suddenly like an imposter; she wanted to cry out, to tell everyone that it was a horrible mistake. But before panic could overtake her, Jentessa caught her gaze—Jentessa with the calming eyes—and it was all right again.

"In the beginning," the Holy Intermediator began, raising her arms to enfold the cavern, "there was Essai, the Maker, at the Center.

"Revolving around the Maker was the Mass, for the Good Earth wasn't firm, then, as it is now, but blended with the waters, the air, the sun, moon, and the stars into one body and spun chaotically in the Void. The Maker gave Order to the Mass, pulling the soil around Itself, and creating a sphere of land. Essai separated the water also, forming the River and streams, and causing lush vegetation to grow. Essai caused the fiery sun to light up the days, and the moon and the stars to brighten the nights; and when all the elements were put in the Order, the Maker caused the creatures to evolve, populating the globe with the fish, the birds, and the animals.

"To keep watch over the Good Earth, Essai sent out upon the surface Its children spirits—ten in all—and after giving them mortal form, divided them into two genders so that they might multiply and know the many sensations that the new world offered. The Maker sent these Half-Divines, led by Phameena and Veer, to found a Colony where they could live out their lives in their bodies and then return to live with It forever in the Center. And so the children went forth across the world,

114

until they found a beautiful land, nestled between Green Mountains, and beside the broad, rushing River. They called this bright place the Melde, because it showed in its beauty the perfection that came from the new-ordered melding of the Mass.

"When the Half-Divines settled this Colony and showed the Maker that it was good, Essai told them to forge two Amulets from the iron of the mountains—an Oval for the women, and a Rectangle for the men—to insure that both genders would be given the right to rule, and to live in peace. Within these irons are the blessing of the Maker, and they have been passed down for generation upon generation, to secure, with each succession, the promise of earthly prosperity.

"As it was for the first Colonists, so it is today." And here Jentessa lifted the Oval Amulet from around Zessiper's bowed head, and held it high. "The passing and the promise continue," she declared and, turning to Paragrin, placed the Amulet around her neck. "As it was for Tempira, as it was for Zessiper, as it was for the race of women rulers back to Phameena the Half-Divine, so it is for you. Hail, Paragrin. Hail, the new Ruler of the Melde!"

The cave was hushed, and everyone within it bowed low.

Jentessa, lowering her arms again to her sides, smiled. "It is done," she said, and Paragrin, gazing out on her silent people, felt very proud.

19

At the feast following the ceremony, everyone sat in the central chamber and gorged themselves; at the end of it all when they were taking the cakes and the wine, Zessiper, her face flushed with drink, rose unsteadily to her feet to make a toast to the great event. She opened her mouth to speak, but as her eyes ran across the crowd of people before her, she was suddenly struck dumb. Her eyes flashed. "What is the meaning of this?" she demanded.

Paragrin looked up at her, surprised.

"It is as you wished, my leader," said Jentessa quietly. "All were to be present."

"You twist my words," said Zessiper. "You knew I would never consent to this—this sacrilege of having *men* present!"

And then Paragrin saw, sitting in a shadowy corner of the room, her old companions. Each had a cake in his hand, but had frozen, alarmed to be so unexpectedly at the center of attention.

"They saw the ceremony?"

"They did."

"And have also joined in our feast, I see."

Cam quickly put down his cake.

"They have."

"I will not permit this!" Zessiper cried. "How dare you take the power into your own hands, Jentessa. Atanelle! Remove them at once. Make them suffer for what they have seen!"

"Stay." Jentessa's voice was even and determined, an equal match to Zessiper's angry cries, and the warriors hesitated in front of the boys, who had risen, panicked, to protect themselves. "Remember, my leader," she said, "that it is no longer you who decides who will remain and who will go. The Amulet of the Maker's blessing now rests on another's shoulders. It is she," Jentessa concluded, looking down to Paragrin, "who must decide."

All eyes turned then to the new Ruler. Paragrin, glancing uneasily from Zessiper to her friends, got to her feet.

"Surely you see the sacrilege?" Zessiper exclaimed. "This ceremony is no place for men."

Paragrin nodded. After all her grandmother had told her, surely this time was a sacred one for the women; they had waited so long. She turned, hesitant, to hear Jentessa, but the woman said, "I offer no persuasion, my young leader; it's your decision." No persuasion! Jentessa's bright eyes only burned into hers, saying more than any words possibly could.

"Paragrin!" Zessiper cried. "Remember what I told you. Men aren't to be trusted. They're evil!"

"But these are my *friends*."

"No man can be a friend," her grandmother returned. "I've learned that lesson well enough; so did your mother . . ." Zessiper laid her hands against the girl's face, and turned it toward herself. "Remember, Paragrin—my Own," she whispered, "what they did to your mother."

"Paragrin." Jentessa's voice pressed into her. "Look at them. Look at the boys."

"No," she breathed, "I can't."

"Look at them!" Jentessa demanded, and frightened, Paragrin raised her eyes to see . . . Cam. He looked so pale, so full of dread. And why? Because of *her*?

Atanelle, taking her silence as an answer, moved forward with the warriors. Cam reached out to block Kerk from their spears, but Atanelle caught Cam's arms and twisted them hard behind his back. He cried out in pain.

"Let him go!" Paragrin commanded, and Atanelle, stunned, released him.

"No!" cried the old ruler. "Don't you realize how dangerous they are? Your mother was murdered!"

"By Trag, not by them," Paragrin returned. "Please, Grandmother, they're my friends! They don't deserve this. They've helped me."

"Helped you!" Zessiper spat.

"It's true!" said Paragrin. "And that should warrant

118

our protection now!" She was silent for a moment, then looked to Jentessa, who stood quietly beside her. "But even without that," she said, "our Holy Intermediator, the closest link we have to the Maker, has told us that the women's ceremony was never supposed to be held separate from the men's; she told us that it represents a promise not just to us women, but to the men, as well. As a ruler, my duty is to follow the Maker's plan, isn't it?" She looked to Zessiper, but the old leader gave no answer. "They stay," she concluded. "They are *welcome* to stay." And with that, she sat down and finished off her wine in one draught.

Zessiper was silent and after a moment sat down again beside her. The warriors returned to their places; so did Jentessa, who tried hard to control the broad smile that threatened, at any second, to emerge. But Cam was not so subtle; he remained standing long after everyone else, and stared at Paragrin with such blatant admiration that the new Ruler of the Melde blushed as red as the wine.

20

When the remains of the feast were being cleared away, Paragrin excused herself from her still speechless grandmother and walked over to the boys.

"Congratulations, Little Gret," said Kerk with a smile, "that was something!" He moved forward to take her hand, but his step faltered, and Cam caught his arm to keep him from falling.

"You need to rest," said Paragrin.

"I won't go back to a prison."

"You won't have to," she said, and turned toward the warriors, who were clustered together a little apart from where she stood. "Atanelle!"

The warrior looked up, surprised, and after a second, came forward, eying the young men suspiciously.

"Atanelle, there's going to be a change in plan," said

Paragrin. "Since these men are no longer prisoners, their room will no longer be a prison. I want you to remove the gate permanently from the doorway and see that they get the rug and extra chair that are in the storage room."

Atanelle shot a look to Zessiper.

"Is something wrong?" asked Paragrin.

Zessiper stared back, but said nothing. "No, my Ruler," said Atanelle, "but if you want my opinion—"

"There will be times when I need it," interrupted Paragrin, "but this isn't one of them."

The warrior studied her in silence; then she bowed and, turning on her heel, marched off toward the prison.

"That's the way!" said Kerk, and grinned.

"Why don't you two go with her?" said Paragrin. "Make sure she gives you that rug."

"All right." Cam beamed at her. "Thank you. . . ."

Paragrin turned to him, but being unable, somehow, to say any more, she simply nodded, and the boys followed Atanelle out into the passage.

"So," said Zessiper at last, coming to stand by her granddaughter's side. "How does it feel to be Ruler?"

Paragrin turned, and thought for a moment before she answered. "It has its advantages," she said, "but I never wanted to be your enemy."

"How could we be enemies?" said Zessiper. "We're family."

"But you must think I'm going to be bad at all this."

The old leader shook her head. "No. In fact, you'll be fine. You carry yourself well, the women seem to respect you, and," she added, "you're not afraid to speak your mind. But that's not surprising; you're my blood, after all. No, your only folly lies in your ignorance of men, but you're young, and for now your leniency should be harmless. They certainly can't try to escape, now that winter's come. And I'll be here to watch them in the cave. Especially that tall one . . ." Paragrin glanced at her, seeing the hardness in her eyes. "I don't like him," said Zessiper.

Paragrin looked away.

"But enough for now," said the old Ruler. "Here, you left this on the floor." She held out the light-colored cape.

"No, you keep that," said the girl, and smiled. "I've got this," and she touched the Oval against her chest.

"Indeed you do," said Zessiper, and squeezing her hand, left her.

At length the room was deserted, and Paragrin, helping herself to a half-empty jug, wandered out into the tunnels. They were quiet now and peaceful, and as she walked toward the entrance to the cave, she mused on all the day's events. "And to think that this morning I was nothing," she thought. The air at the entrance rushed up at her, cold and strong, but it felt good against her flushed skin; and she looked out at the snowy earth content, thinking how beautifully the white ice sparkled in the moonlight.

"Paragrin?"

She turned, surprised. "Cam!"

"I couldn't sleep," he said, coming to stand before

her. "Is it all right if I stay here for a moment?"

"Of course."

"It's been so long since I've been outside. My Maker, look at all that snow! I'm glad we're not out in it anymore."

"Me, too," said the girl.

"Paragrin," said Cam, after a second had passed, "I can't begin to tell you how amazed I am by everything that's happened to you. Everything Jentessa said about there being two Rulers—it sounds fantastic, yet somehow I believe it. I mean, if Jentessa says it's true; and besides, it makes so much *sense*."

Paragrin gazed at him.

"And Trag kept it a secret. . . . How dare he hold our history from us! But, oh, Paragrin," Cam exclaimed, "to think that you're one of the Rulers! That scene at the feast was . . . well, amazing. I can't tell you how impressed I am by what you did."

Paragrin colored again.

"And I'm not saying that just because it saved Kerk and me," he said, "but because it must not have been easy for you to do, especially with Zessiper standing right there. It was just—just amazing."

Paragrin looked down to her boots, to the snow, anywhere but to him. "It was really not so hard," she muttered.

There was silence for a moment, then Cam reached out with his hand. "The Amulet—may I touch it?" he asked.

"Oh, certainly." She held it out for him.

"It feels so important," Cam said, smiling, "so

heavy . . ." His fingers brushed against Paragrin's. She gazed at them, alarmed, a surge of excitement sweeping through her body. He wrapped his fingers gently around hers, the iron still enclosed.

"Paragrin!"

She pulled away. Zessiper stood at the entrance, her eyes glinting in the moonlight.

"What do you think you're doing?" she demanded, advancing on Cam. "You've no right to touch that Oval, and no right to touch that woman. She's not a common girl you find in the street, she's a Ruler!"

"I—I didn't mean any disrespect," stammered Cam.

"Get away from here, back to your pretty little brother, before I let my good sense get the better of me and throw you out to die in the snow."

"Grandmother!" Paragrin exclaimed.

"It's all right," said Cam, his eyes never off Zessiper. "I'll go. I'll see you tomorrow," and he disappeared down the tunnel.

Paragrin gaped at her, speechless.

"Did he hurt you?"

"Of course not!"

"Then it's a good thing I came when I did, isn't it?" said Zessiper. "Here, I wanted to bring you the cape," and she held it out.

"But I said you could keep it, don't you remember?"

"That's right," said the old leader, smiling. "I must have forgotten. Good night, then," and turning, she strode back into the cave.

And Paragrin, left alone again, stared after her.

21

In the morning, Paragrin was more confused than ever about the incident at the entrance. She sat on her bed, her bare feet tucked beneath her, and wondered if she had imagined the whole thing—Cam coming, his hand pressing hers . . . What would have happened if Zessiper hadn't appeared? She shook her head, too embarrassed to think any more about it, and hoped sincerely that she could avoid seeing him that day—and Zessiper, too.

But that last wish was quickly broken. Jentessa came into the room soon afterward with an invitation to take breakfast with Zessiper in the old Ruler's chamber.

"There are many things to discuss," said the woman, and Paragrin, suspecting that Jentessa already knew of her impropriety, reluctantly pulled on her boots to follow, fearing the worst.

Yet Zessiper bore no reproach for the evening before. She didn't even mention it; her thoughts had turned—as Paragrin was ashamed *hers* hadn't—to more important matters.

"Now, my Own," said Zessiper, putting aside her bowl, "the time has come to decide our plan of attack for returning the Oval to power."

" 'Attack'—if necessary," put in Jentessa.

"Do you think there's any other way?" returned the old Ruler. "You know Trag. He's not a man of subtleties. If we threaten his hold on the Melde, he'll not sit idle. Neither can we." She looked to Paragrin. "Don't you agree?"

"Yes, but I don't see how we can defeat him by force," said the young leader. "He has his troops, after all."

"So do we."

"Yes, but women against men . . ."

"Who flipped whom into the snow?" said Jentessa with a smile.

"But Kerk was weak. It wasn't a fair test."

"Atanelle can fight anyone," said Zessiper. "She's strong as a bear."

"Our strength won't lie in our muscles, but in our unique way of fighting," said Jentessa. "Atanelle's method is based on balance and quickness. The smallest of us, with its mastery, should be able not only to attack, but to defend herself against the mightiest of men."

"If it's really as effective as you say," said Paragrin, "we must all certainly become masters. Can Atanelle teach her fighting?"

"She can."

126

"Then we'll have classes here in the cave, and practice night and day if we have to, to be ready." She took a breath. "I guess we should set out as early as spring?"

"The sooner the better," said Zessiper.

"There is a more pressing need for going in the spring than you realize, my young leader," said Jentessa. "Tell me, what exactly happened in the Melde that night you were there? Why were you forced to leave?"

"Well, Kerk brought attention to us, and Trag learned then that we were from Lexterre."

"And that's why you fled?"

"Yes."

"And why you were pursued?"

Paragrin looked to her, sharply. "How did you know we were followed?"

Jentessa didn't answer. "Is that why you were pursued?" she repeated.

Paragrin studied her, trying hard to penetrate her thoughts; but beyond the insistent eyes, the woman was, as usual, inscrutable. "No," she said at last, "at least, I don't think so. I think we were followed because of me. When he saw my face, he was frightened. . . . He called me Tempira."

"The villain," Zessiper breathed.

"Still, a resemblance is no reason to send out men in the worst storm of the year," said Jentessa.

"There may be one other reason," said Paragrin. "I didn't think much of it at the time, but the laces of my jacket, they pulled apart when I fought him. It may be that—that the iron showed through."

Zessiper's eyes widened.

127

"Now for *that*," Jentessa concluded, "he would follow you through earth and rock."

"Then it's especially lucky I escaped," said Paragrin. "I'm safe here. He doesn't know where to look for me. He'll just assume I went back to Lexterre, and"— she caught her breath, horrified—"and go there!"

"Precisely," said Jentessa. "In fact, he's already tried. Fortunately, the snow proved as troublesome for him as it did for you."

"How do you *know* all this?" cried Paragrin.

"Just accept it," said Zessiper, frowning. "In all the years I've known her, she's never been wrong. It's one of her more annoying traits."

"Thank you," said Jentessa. "But regardless, you see that this spring will be a special one for Trag, as well. He's stopped for now; but he hasn't given up. He'll go to your village as soon as he's able, with well-armed soldiers in tow."

"To find the Oval," said Paragrin.

Jentessa nodded. "And you. He knows who you are, now."

"His daughter," said Paragrin miserably.

"*Tempira's* daughter," said Zessiper, and squeezed her hand.

"That's right." And Paragrin smiled. "Well, I won't disappoint his fear. We'll get to Lexterre before him, and have our meeting there."

"That's better anyway," said Zessiper. "He won't know the land any more than we do. Our chances for victory have now improved."

"And after this victory," said Paragrin, "what then?"

128

"Then," said Zessiper, rising to her feet, "after we have avenged our dear Tempira's death by disposing of both him *and* his idiot father, ah! then . . ." she looked down at Paragrin, beaming, "then, my Own, you will rule in the only perfect way—*alone!*"

"Never! You know there must be a man to rule beside her," Jentessa declared, "or the Melde shall be just as corrupt as it is now."

The old Ruler spun about, and Paragrin read the indignation in her face, as if she were saying "That, it could never be!"

"I said it in jest," Zessiper replied coolly. "There's no need to scold me, Jentessa; I know very well what the Maker demands. You've been reminding me of it for forty years."

"I lose my patience for jesting," Jentessa returned, "when the Maker is concerned."

"So I've noticed," snapped Zessiper, and the two fell silent. Paragrin looked from one to the other uneasily.

"Well, I've work to do," said the old Ruler at last. "I'll oversee the making of weapons and clothes for traveling—if you will permit me, Paragrin."

"Of course," said the girl.

"While I'm doing that," she concluded, "I would suggest that you get better acquainted with our faithful but austere Holy Intermediator, who will teach you and keep after you about what is right and wrong toward the fulfillment of the Maker's plan; which often includes," she said, turning again on Jentessa, "trying to dissuade you from doing what you know to be *just*"; and she knocked her bowl away with her boot and left them both, her heavy stride sending echoes through the tunnel.

Paragrin watched her go, and looked anxiously for Jentessa's response. The woman's face was calm, but her eyes, betraying her rage, were flashing.

22

Another storm blew across the land, sending snow twisting through the air and charging to the forests. The wind howled; the River, its waters pierced with cold, flowed sluggishly between its frosted banks. Everywhere the heavy hand of winter retook its toll and warned the creatures of the forest and village alike to keep to their homes.

At Lexterre, when the white morning sky cleared to an icy blue, Strap ventured forth with his men to return the town to order; while the women, their girls gathered around them, stayed indoors and wove more coverings for the beds.

At the Melde Trag leaned toward the hearth and, rubbing his bulky hands together, cursed the cold; while his people, huddled in their houses, took what nourishment they could from the meager supplies and cursed him.

And at the cave, layers of heavy skins were hung in front of the entrance, so that throughout the hidden settlement the tunnels and chambers were kept warm. The Ductae, under Zessiper's watchful eye, busied themselves preparing clothing for the journey ahead while Jentessa took Paragrin under her private care and spent hours, as the young leader listened attentively, relating her stories of the Melde religion and of the long and honorable history of the people.

While Paragrin was occupied, though, Kerk was not. Still a prisoner of sorts in the confines of the cave, he spent his time pacing the passages and staring gloomily out at the snow. Then one day he noticed that three of the women were staring at him during dinner, and from that moment on he found new meaning to his life with the Ductae. After only a few days of trying, he'd collected around him a steady clutch of admirers— including the warrior Bodurtha—who were eager to learn those parts of growing up they had missed. He was only too happy to teach them.

Paragrin watched his turnabout, and wondered anxiously if Cam would follow his lead. He certainly had his opportunities, yet the tall young man smiled suggestively at no one. He *talked* to the women, especially to the older ones, and asked them questions about their lives' experiences. They were glad to have someone take such an interest in the stories that had long since grown old, and Cam's unassuming manner soon won him a special place among the Ductae.

132

Jentessa liked him, and to Paragrin's delight invited him to take part in their private discussions. It did seem odd that he was given as much attention as *she*—after all, it was her duty to learn the history, not his—but he became such a worthy partner, both as a rival in debate and as a gleeful accomplice against Jentessa, that Paragrin soon forgot her puzzlement. Besides, whenever the Holy Intermediator grew long-winded, as she often did, there were always those fine green eyes to look into; and since they were very often gazing back into hers, she found many opportunities.

Zessiper watched them, her gray eyes fixed first shrewdly on Jentessa, then falling like iron weights onto Cam. He shrank beneath them and, when he felt their burden, would excuse himself from the company and move on to a more solitary occupation; and when he did, Zessiper, too, would move on.

Paragrin dreaded these silent assaults as much as he did, the memory of Zessiper's threat still hanging in her mind; yet for all of her desire to save Cam from the old Ruler's hate, she was just as leery of confronting her. Zessiper's love for Paragrin was strong, stronger than anything the girl had known, and she wanted desperately to justify the trust; yet as time passed, she found it more and more difficult. Zessiper was changing; *she* was changing; the difference in their views widened rather than narrowed; and Paragrin began to feel uncomfortable with the old leader's confidence.

"Jentessa is an interesting woman," her grandmother allowed during one of their special talks, "and a kind and good one, of course, but I'll confess to you that

I'm finding her sermons a little tiring. They're always so strict and righteous, don't you think?"

Paragrin smiled noncommittally, and Zessiper laughed. "Oh, I used to be in awe of her too, when I was young. There she was, this strange girl who seemed to appear from nowhere right after the separation, so bright and serious and calm. I made her Holy Intermediator myself, you know." She shook her head. "But I lose patience, now. Jentessa has no passion in her, no fury for the injustices done to us. Ah, but you"—and here Zessiper smiled triumphantly—"you're my Own. You're like *me*." And with that, she strode away, well satisfied with their alliance, and left Paragrin to sit by herself—and wonder.

23

The weeks wore on, and even Zessiper—her ambition for a time forgotten—fell into the blissful tranquility that settled over the land; for it was the month of deepest winter, when the snow lay still and solid on the earth.

It was the time of the Winter Festival, and at Lexterre, the girls danced again before the young men—all except for Ellagette, who, with the object of her affection gone, found her interest in the gaiety dimmed. At evening, when the fires blazed in the square, Strap gathered the town together, and they all gave thanks to Him.

At the Colony, the Festival was officially forgotten—again. Those pious people who remembered the old ways were made to honor Essai quietly in their own homes, without ever having their hearts lifted by seeing how many other followers there still were in the old city.

But in the cave, there was great celebration. Everyone collected with Jentessa in the sacred chamber to praise the Maker and afterward retired to the central room to feast. When the dinner was finished, the musicians brought forth their instruments and performed more of the haunting melodies they had played before. They sang, too, in delicate harmonies, and filled the cave with music.

Cam sat apart from Paragrin—for Zessiper was beside her—and listened, mesmerized, to the voices. He rocked gently, moving his lips to the words that they sang. Jentessa watched him and when the song was done, said aloud, "Once Paragrin told me, Cam, that you have quite a beautiful voice."

Both companions colored, she staring intently at the floor, and he casting a glance to Kerk, who looked up, his attention diverted from the young women at his side.

"I don't sing," said Cam quietly.

"Of course you do," Jentessa said with a smile. "We've all heard you humming to yourself when you didn't think anyone was listening."

The women laughed, and Cam blushed again.

"Well, I'm not supposed . . . in Lexterre, we don't—" he began.

"I know," Jentessa interrupted, "in Lexterre, men aren't supposed to sing. Ridiculous! They can have the most marvelous depth to their voices. Won't you grace us with yours? A great many here have never heard a man sing before."

Zessiper's gaze hardened, but the Ductae clapped their hands and pleaded for Cam to join in. He glanced again at Kerk; and Kerk, seeing him weaken, cast aside

136

the women about him and stalked from the room.

Cam's shoulders fell; Paragrin watched him, fearing that even here, he would bow to his brother's scorn. Yet Jentessa laid her hand upon him, saying softly, "You are far from Lexterre now, my friend."

He turned and looked at her. "You're right," he said at last. "I *will* sing if you'd like, but I can only do 'Beneath the Fair Green Mountains.' Do you know it?"

"Naturally," she said, and signaled the musicians to begin the melody.

Cam glanced nervously about him; then, closing his eyes, began—the lyrics rising deep from within his chest and floating out into the cave. The Ductae listened, enthralled; while Paragrin, her head fallen to one side, was there again on the banks of the River, hearing—for the first wonderful time—his song.

Around the corner of the tunnel, hidden in shadow, Kerk lingered; and when his brother had finished, and the chamber rang with applause, he smiled.

Then the horror of his own response swept over him. He turned and ran through the tunnels to the entrance, throwing aside the animal skins to confront the snow.

It lay there still, deep and impassable, and striking the ice with his foot, he slouched by the wall, scowling.

And Cam, back in the chamber, sang again that night.

The weeks passed, and as the season slowly began to change, so did the peaceful atmosphere of the cave. While the women started to craft the weaponry, Zessiper and Jentessa sat with Paragrin to lay the final plans for their return.

"As much as I've become part of the Ductae," said

the young leader, looking away from the others, "there's something that I want to—that I feel I must—do by myself."

"You won't confront Trag," said Zessiper, "not without me there."

"No, not that," said Paragrin, turning again to face them. "But I do want to go to the village first—by myself."

"Without the boys, even, as companions?" asked Jentessa.

"Oh, with them, of course."

"If they can go with you, why can't we?" Zessiper demanded.

"Because Lexterre is their home . . . and my home," said Paragrin. "I've had my troubles there. I need to face these people again, and convince them to respect me now, as a leader. I don't want to arrive with an army behind me, as if I were taking the village by force. Can you understand? This is especially important because of Strap. He's my brother, after all—*half* brother—and he may rule beside me one day." She paused, adding in a lower voice, "We have a lot to discuss before you arrive."

"I understand," said Jentessa, "and I think it will not endanger anything if you leave early. You seem to feel the need to prove something to those people."

Paragrin nodded.

"But remember, my young ruler, that the respect of leadership is not won with Amulets any more than armies. Those troubles that you spoke of—the people of Lexterre aren't the only ones who will have to change. You, too, must compromise."

138

Paragrin looked at her warily, but Zessiper laughed. "Nonsense," she said, clasping her granddaughter about the shoulders, "they'll never know the wind that hit them."

24

In three days, Jentessa had said, the companions could leave for Lexterre; but Kerk cared little for other people's decisions. He was anxious to go and now that the snow had begun to melt, he was determined to leave on the morrow.

"I wish you'd come with me," he said to his brother, as they stood that evening at the entrance.

Zessiper, who had started for the entrance herself, stopped in the shadows of the tunnel when she saw them, and listened.

"And I wish you'd go back·to the village," Cam returned.

"Oh, I just don't see the sense in it," said Kerk. "I mean, it's stupid, Lexterre standing up against Trag."

"We'll have the Ductae."

140

"They won't make any difference and you know it. Come on, Partner, if you go with me to the Melde, we'll have a fine time! My Maker, you'll end up there anyway, and how would you like to arrive, as an adventurer looking for fun, or as a prisoner?"

"This fight is important, Kerk," came the reply.

"Ah, I don't even know you anymore! We used to be such fellows together. Now you sing, and spend all your time talking with women. What hold do these people have on you, anyway?"

Cam was silent for a moment, then glanced across at him, smiling.

"What's wrong with you?" said Kerk.

"I think," Cam began, looking down again, "no, I'm certain that I . . . I . . ."

"You . . . you . . . what?"

Cam took a deep breath. "Paragrin," he said.

"Paragrin *what*?"

"She's . . . she's very special to me."

"What do you mean, 'special'?"

"Rot it, I'm in love with her!" Cam exclaimed, reddening. "Does everything have to be drawn out for you?"

"Great Father Divine," said Kerk.

Zessiper's eyes smoldered in the darkness.

"I want her to be my mate. I'm going to ask her to be Joined with me."

"Great Father Divine," said Kerk again.

"Is that all you're going to say?"

"What else can I say? But Partner . . . are you sure she'll accept you?"

"Of course I'm not sure! But I think she will.

We've"—he smiled again—"we've never really said anything to each other, and yet, when I look into her eyes, I see such . . . such . . ."

"Such what?"

"Such . . . hope. Such . . . excitement, toward *me*!"

Kerk stared at him. "Well, I think I understand things better now. Just as well I'm not going on your little journey home, isn't it?"

Cam said nothing.

"Well then, I'll go say good-bye to Little Gr—to Paragrin. I'll see you back at our room afterward, all right?"

Cam broke from his dream, frowning. "You'd better not tell her anything," he warned.

"Not a thing. I promise!"

"All right then," said Cam. "I'll be waiting for you."

Zessiper turned and stole down the tunnel; and Kerk, flashing a confident grin, sauntered away.

But Kerk's smile faded when he was out of his brother's sight. What horrible embarrassment was Cam setting himself up for, anyway? It had been clear from the start which of the two of them she preferred. Not that he didn't wish it were the other way around; after all, *he* had no interest in Paragrin. And yet, a girl's feelings were deep; unlike men, they set their hearts on one person. How could he ever let her know—gently—that it was impossible? And yet he must, for Cam's sake. This visit had to be quick—and final.

He came at last to her room and looked inside. She was there at the mirror, working up her hair to a pretty fashion. He shook his head sadly and slapped the stone.

Paragrin spun about, but seeing it was only him,

turned again to the mirror. "Oh, hello, Kerk," she said. "What do you want? I'm busy."

"Yes, I see," he said, coming to stand behind her. "You look nice."

She glanced at him suspiciously. "So," she said after a minute, "let me guess why you've come. You're not going to Lexterre with Cam and me, are you?"

"No, I'm not," said Kerk.

"Why aren't I surprised?" she sighed. "What are you going to do, stay here and see how many more of the Ductae you can add to your list?"

"No, I'm off to the Melde. Tomorrow. Not that I want to get away from you, or from any of the other girls, you understand."

"Of course not," said Paragrin.

"In fact, I've just come to say good-bye."

"Good-bye, then," said Paragrin.

"I wish I could convince you and Cam not to join in this ridiculous battle," he continued, "you'll only make things harder for yourselves, but since you're determined all I can do is wish you luck. So—" he turned her from the mirror, "good luck!"

His hands slid to her waist, and to Paragrin's great astonishment, he pulled her close against his body. A sudden surge of the old feeling came over her, and she trembled, hovering between a longing for his kiss and a fear of his touch. His lips came nearer to hers; she stood, horrified, bracing herself for the final moment, when Kerk, in deference to his brother, shifted at the last second and pecked her on the cheek.

"So!" he said, releasing her. "That's that! Good-bye." And well satisfied with his sacrifice, he left her.

Paragrin glared after him, too angry to speak; then the old feeling fell away as easily as it had come. She remembered herself and, turning again to the mirror, thought of better things.

Cam strolled down the passageway to his room, thinking how lucky it was that Kerk wouldn't be joining them on the journey home. What happy prospects it now held! Alone with Paragrin for a number of days—what better time to confess his love. To think that soon he might take her into his arms; and, if all went well, kiss her!

With that cheerful thought in mind, he entered his chamber, but halfway across the floor, he stopped. His skin started to tingle; he felt uneasy, as if someone were— He spun around. There, standing by the torch, was Zessiper. He stepped back, pressing his hands against his legs to keep them from shaking.

"What are you doing here?" he demanded. "What do you want?"

"Victory," said Zessiper, and was silent again.

"For your people? Of course," said Cam, "so do I want victory. I despise Trag as much as Paragrin does."

"How could you?" Zessiper breathed, moving out from the wall. "Your people haven't suffered. Your mother wasn't murdered by his hands."

"No," said Cam, stepping back again, "but I can understand how—"

"You understand nothing! If you truly understood," said the old Ruler, "you would leave this place and stop interfering with her evolution."

"Interfering? How am I interfering?" Cam exclaimed.

"Great Maker, I've hardly touched her since that night at the entrance!"

"With my good vigilance, you haven't," said Zessiper, "but I know you; you think your time has come. *Now*, when she needs most to appear strong and independent!"

"She *is* strong," said Cam. "She's proven that."

"Her trials have just begun," returned the woman. "These past few months have been a practice only to a willing audience. Now the time of battle is nearly upon us. Her mind must be clear, purposeful. Paragrin barely knows what she is; you know not at all: a leader, chosen by Essai to rule over all. Sweet Maker, she's practically divine! And you would lure her away, take advantage of her innocence, rob her of her dignity."

"No! You don't know me," Cam said. "I could never hurt her. I *love* her!"

"You don't know love!" Zessiper cried, seizing him. "You give nothing, only lust. *I* love! I give friendship and caring! I watch over, and support her in what she does; you would force her to *choose*."

"I wouldn't!" Cam exclaimed, pulling from her hold.

"Not openly, but inwardly," said Zessiper, her hard gray eyes grasping him still, "she would have to choose between you and her sacred duty to the Oval."

"That's not true! You're only saying that because you don't like me."

"I hate you," returned the Ruler, "but above all, I fear you. With the hold you have on Paragrin, you're even more dangerous than Trag."

145

Cam stared at her, unable to look away, to close his eyes and ears to her presence.

"Can you deny that these feelings you've stirred in her draw her apart from the mission? No, of course you can't. And if you care for her half as much as you claim to, get away, *now*! Go with your brother tomorrow to the Colony, and stay there. We don't want you. It's not your war!"

Cam said nothing, and Zessiper put out her hand to his shoulder. "For Paragrin's sake, I've given you this chance to leave," she said quietly. "I think you've seen my point. This time tomorrow, you'll have ceased to be a problem . . . one way or another."

She turned and was gone; and Cam stood alone in the room, still seeing her.

25

"Partner, what are you doing hunched in the corner?"

Cam started, surprised to have the silence so suddenly broken.

"I've just said good-bye to Little Gret," said Kerk, sitting down beside him. "Everything's set. You'll have a fine time with her on the journey home."

"I can't go," said Cam.

"What do you mean, you can't go? I thought it was all decided."

He shook his head. "I never really realized how important her mission was, how important *she* was."

"Ho! That's all you've been telling me for months."

"No, can't you see? For me to try to claim her for my own, why, it's terrible! Selfish. I could ruin everything."

147

"What are you talking about? What could you possibly ruin by loving her?"

"Ah, Kerk, you don't understand!" Cam exclaimed, getting to his feet. "My love is unimportant. This battle is all that matters. Paragrin can't waste her time on me. Oh, why didn't I see this sooner?"

"Your mind's gone soft," Kerk retorted. " 'This battle is all that matters.' You sound like the old she-wolf."

"Maybe she has a point," Cam said, turning on him. "You're not the only one with answers!"

"Steady, now, Partner, don't yell at me. I don't care what you do. Go talk to Little Gret. She's the one you have to convince."

Cam hesitated, pulling at his jacket. "All right, I will," he said, "and I won't be long." He disappeared down the passageway, with Kerk left frowning behind him.

When Cam came to her room, he stood a moment in the doorway, watching as she wove a brightly colored ribbon through her hair. For a second, his resolution faltered; every excuse he could think of for staying by her side rushed to his mind; but Zessiper's words came back to haunt him, and when Paragrin turned, he was determined again.

"Cam!" The bloom rose in her cheeks. "I was just going to find you."

"Were you?" He forced his gaze from her face.

"What's wrong? Does my hair look that bad? I was only having fun; it's been so many months since it's been long enough to braid."

"Nothing's wrong," said Cam, pulling again at his

148

jacket, "but I do think you might have spent your time on something less . . . frivolous."

"I hardly ever indulge myself with styling," she said in a small voice. "Back in Lexterre, it was all Aridda could do, to make me—"

"You're not in Lexterre now!" Cam charged. "You're not the same person you were back there. If you were, then . . . then it would all be different. But you're a ruler now, and you can't waste your time . . ." he fought for his words, ". . . playing with braids!"

"What's wrong with you?" Paragrin said. "I've never heard you talk like this."

"Why does everyone think I'm wrong but me?" Cam returned. "Why am I the only one of us who finally sees the danger? Paragrin, I *do* care about the battle with Trag. I want the Oval to be restored!"

"Of course you do. I know that."

"But if we don't change our ways, it may never happen! The smallest thing could tip the scales. Paragrin, you'll be fighting for your life out there!—for the lives of your women, for the fates of everyone. Every thought, every motion of yours has to be bent toward gaining that victory."

"How dare you accuse me of neglecting my duty!" Paragrin cried. "I know very well what's at stake."

"Then act like you do, rot it all," said Cam, "and stop wasting your time on *me*."

They fell silent, confronting each other; then, seeing the hurt in her eyes, he looked away again.

"Wasting my time?" she echoed. "Cam, what are you saying?"

149

"I'm sorry, Paragrin; it's my fault, not yours. I was the selfish one, taking you apart from your mission."

"Who put you up to this kind of talk?" she demanded. "Who said I was neglecting my duty? Zessiper? Has she been telling you our friendship is interfering? You know how one-sided she is!"

"It doesn't matter. She's right this time . . . isn't she?"

"But I haven't neglected anything. Every thought, every motion . . ." Her voice fell away, her fingers slowly twisting around the ribbon in her hair.

"I'll leave with Kerk tomorrow," he said softly. "I won't bother you anymore."

"But how can it be wrong to care for someone?" she implored. "Is that what wearing this Oval means? That we have to keep apart? If it does, then I don't want it!"

"Don't say that," Cam cried. "Paragrin! You were *chosen*."

She looked to him, frightened. "I—I didn't mean it."

He stared at her. "I'm so sorry," he whispered, and ran from the room.

And Paragrin stood apart, trembling, the iron clasped to her heart.

The morning came, gray and dreary. The Ductae gathered at the entrance to say farewell to the two young men who had become their friends. Kerk's clutch of admirers hovered about him, and told him how much he would be missed.

"I'll see you all again," he promised, "when you come to the Melde." And then, thinking under what circum-

150

stances that might be, he regretted saying it.

Paragrin leaned against the wall of the entrance and stared blankly into the crowd of women still waving good-bye.

"Why, what's wrong?" asked Jentessa, as she came up beside her. "Am I too late? Has Kerk left yet?"

"Yes," she answered. "They're both gone, now."

"Both?"

"Of course," she returned. "I can't have Cam to worry about, can I? I have a job to do." And she walked back into the cave.

Jentessa watched her go, astonished, then turned to stare at the empty path the boys had taken. By now the crowd was thinning, and the women drifted past her into the tunnel; but she was not the only one left outside. There was one other, lingering. Jentessa moved her gaze and a sharp chill ran through her body. Zessiper turned, her shining eyes meeting instantly with hers; the two women looked at each other in silence, then the old Ruler broke into a triumphant smile, and strode past Jentessa into the cave.

26

The rain beat down against the mountainside. Paragrin stood in the entranceway and watched the water form rivers in the snow that remained. It was late, but the sun, hidden behind the clouds, was just setting. She pushed her hair impatiently from her face.

Tomorrow she would begin her four-day journey back to Lexterre. Jentessa was showing signs of worry: she had advised that the Ductae follow *two* days after Paragrin left, instead of three; and she had told the young leader to take the trail marked in the woods, and avoid the long path of the River. She had been to the village herself, the woman had said, and Paragrin had accepted that. Nothing really surprised her anymore. All she knew was that they were running out of time.

She tried that evening to remember how it had felt,

those many weeks before, when she stood breathless in the sacred chamber accepting the Oval. Had it been pride, excitement, anticipation of glory? She felt none of them now; only fear, and a strong sense of inadequacy. The confrontation with Trag, she could still just barely comprehend; the reunion with Strap and his people seemed much too real. She had been so important at the cave, so respected; to go back now alone—truly alone—to the town that had banished her was all very hard. She had thought once to change her plan, to go with the Ductae; but that part of her that needed proof before remained and called her coward. She would go back alone; but more to show something to herself now than to Lexterre.

She turned from the rain to her bed.

In the morning, the young Ruler stood before her mirror for the last time. She wished that she could have seen a heroine there, a great and courageous woman like Phameena the Half-Divine, someone who set out to change the world and thought nothing of it; but despite the grand appearance of the Amulet against her chest, she saw no one but herself. Defeated, she took the iron from around her neck; and it was then that she saw Atanelle standing in the doorway.

"What do you want?" she demanded, slipping the iron into her pocket.

"I've brought your new supply of arrows, my Ruler," the young woman announced, and held them out. "I fashioned them myself, and they're the finest anywhere, I assure you."

Paragrin took and put them on the bed. "Thank you," she said.

The warrior stood there still.

"Was there something else?"

"Oh, no," said Atanelle, shaking her head too many times. "I just came to see if—say, that's pretty. Where did this come from?" She bent and retrieved a brightly colored ribbon from the floor.

Paragrin saw it too, and winced.

"I've heard," the warrior continued, her thick fingers fondling the cloth, "that in the old days, girls of the Melde would wind this around their hair." She pulled her braid across her shoulder. "Something like this, tied at the bottom, like—"

"What are you doing?" Paragrin cried.

Atanelle dropped the ribbon.

"The battle may be only days away, and my chief warrior is playing with braids!"

"I—I'm sorry," said the woman, "it's just that I've been . . . well, I've been thinking a great deal about . . . about men."

"Men?" Paragrin echoed.

"Well, for the first time in my life, I'm going to see a lot of them; not just one or two prisoners, but many, living their own lives," said Atanelle. "Great numbers, all at one time!"

"On the battlefield," said Paragrin.

"Yes, but I was thinking of the Melde! My Maker, I've never even been to the Colony, can you imagine? And, oh, if it weren't for you, I might never had gotten a chance to see my real home. If it weren't for you, I don't think I'd ever have known what we were really fighting for, and that—that's really what I came to say."

"What do you mean, you didn't know what we were fighting for?" said Paragrin, after a moment. "It's not a mystery. We just want to return the Oval to power."

". . . alongside the Rectangle," the warrior amended. "I mean, that's the whole point, isn't it? Women *and* men working together?"

Paragrin stared at her.

"I never really understood that, believed that, until you came. Our Glorious Ruler Zessiper, she, well, I suspect she doesn't think much of men," Atanelle whispered. "That kind of togetherness, it isn't her target. You know, I used to think like her. That's why I treated you and your friends so badly at first. But now, well, had I known then what I know now, that men could be so . . . that *some* men could be . . . well, that some men like *Cam* could be . . ."

Paragrin smiled.

"Not that I think anything could happen," the warrior said quickly, twisting her fingers around her braid. "I mean, he never looks at anyone but you, and I would certainly never try to take—even if I had a chance, which I don't even *pretend* to have, but—well, there must be others, right? in the Melde? Seeing the two of you together gave me such hope for this reunion. You seemed so strong together, so happy, like *two* rulers, almost! That emptiness I've seen in your grandmother sometimes, that loneliness, I never saw it in you"—she paused, glancing across to Paragrin—"until now. You don't seem quite as settled anymore, if you don't mind me

155

saying so. Since he left, you don't seem to be concentrating on anything, as if you weren't quite all there. . . ."

"Like the lone woman figure in the mural," said Paragrin quietly.

"Well, that's not alone anymore," said Atanelle.

Paragrin looked at her. "What do you mean, that last figure in the line?"

"Yes, that's the one. It's not alone anymore."

Paragrin's eyes widened, and she went for the door.

"Before you go," said Atanelle, "I just wanted to tell you that everyone will be waiting for you at the entrance, and that, well, I'm just very glad you're our leader now. For you, and for what you represent, I— I'll be proud to offer my life at the battle"—and she went down on one knee before her—"my Glorious Ruler."

Paragrin stared at her. There was the horrible warrior chief in all her belligerent splendor, her knives in her belt, her wooden armor strapped to her chest, and her square head rising just as forcefully as before, and yet . . .

"Thank you," said Paragrin, laying her hand on the woman's broad shoulder. "Please, get up." The warrior obeyed. "I don't think I've ever said . . . Atanelle . . . how grateful I am to you for teaching all of us to defend ourselves. If it weren't for your clever way of fighting, I don't think we'd even have a chance of victory."

The warrior bowed her head.

"But above all," said Paragrin, "I thank you for this talk. You've been more of a friend to me just now than I deserved from you."

The warrior colored, and began to back out into the tunnel.

"Now go," said Paragrin, "and tell all the people that I'll be with them in a few minutes."

"Yes, my Glorious Ruler!" Atanelle exclaimed, and beaming, she hurried away down the passage.

Paragrin watched her disappear, well contented; then she remembered.

"The mural!"

In an instant she was gone, running down the winding tunnels to the sacred chamber. The door was open from Jentessa's room, spilling the light from the crevice across the floor. Paragrin entered and with faltering footsteps approached the mural. Yes! It was true. There beside the lonely woman was a painted man. The picture was complete—except for the absence of a rectangle on the male figure's chest. Paragrin stared at it for several minutes, thoughtful. Then she pulled the Oval Amulet from her pocket and placed it around her neck.

When she came at last to her people at the entrance, Paragrin was ready, her new arrows set firmly into her quiver, her bow and pack of supplies slung across her shoulder. The women were all dressed for battle—a show of united strength arranged by Atanelle for her leave-taking—and their hair was all woven into single fat braids that hung down their backs. Paragrin pushed her own locks from her face and smiled.

Jentessa and Zessiper stood off by themselves, waiting. Paragrin looked to the Intermediator, and the two women spoke to each other in silence; Paragrin asking

157

without words about the meaning in the mural, and Jentessa, her dark eyes shining, answering.

Then Zessiper stepped forward, her face radiant, and held out her arms. Paragrin went to her embrace willingly, feeling in that moment like her granddaughter again. The sense of alliance came rushing back, as it had in the old leader's room so long ago. But Zessiper's eyes burned, and grasping Paragrin's arms with her lean brown hands, she whispered to her ear, "You're my blood, child! You're like *me*."

Paragrin flinched and released her, but the old Ruler stepped back with pride.

"And so," said the new Ruler of the Melde, turning quickly to her people, "the time has come at last. You will never be out of my thoughts."

"We'll see you in six days," said the warrior, "ready to stand again at your side."

"Very well," said Paragrin, "and incidently, Atanelle," she added quietly, drawing the ribbon from her pocket, "they do wear these in their hair; down at the bottom, as you said."

The warrior blushed a very deep shade of pink, and took the ribbon.

"Fare well!" said Paragrin, starting down the path.

"Fare well!" cried the women. "Good steps on your journey!"

"And on yours," she called back; then she slipped out of sight beneath the forest trees, leaving the cave echoing with the cheers of the Ductae behind her.

Zessiper watched her go. "At the battle," she whispered, "we shall meet again, my Own."

158

27

Far from the ominous stirrings in the cave and Colony, Paragrin wound her way up the forest trail toward Lexterre. Two days deep into the wood, she found much time to indulge in the budding of the trees and the sweet new smell of spring as it wafted down from the mountaintops. She even allowed herself to hope, now and then, for a future—beyond the threat of battle—when she might return victorious to the Melde . . . and to Cam.

He was often in her thoughts, and though his absence was keenly felt, she used him then as an extra reason to win against Trag. If she should lose, if the Oval should be taken, she knew she would never see Cam again; there could be no losing for her without dying. That was understood. She wished only that he could be there to tell, and share her fears.

But she bore them alone through that half of the journey, and on the third day, when the sun was just beginning to set, and her mind had begun to turn uneasily to the arrival tomorrow in Lexterre, there came through the air a tune so beautiful and sad that Paragrin stopped in her tracks to listen. Never had a bird sung so wonderfully, and she set off softly through the woods to find it. She strayed from the trail, but didn't think. She was drawn, almost magically, to the music.

She walked on, wondering anew at each step how steady and lasting the song became; not just strings of common notes, but whole measures, and changing. She was so intent upon the sound that it came as a surprise when the sun's watery reflection blinded her through the trees. She stumbled, and broke a branch on the ground.

The music stopped. Paragrin cursed herself, hoping against odds that the bird had not taken flight and would sing again. She held her breath, waiting; and then after a minute the song did begin anew, sweetly, softly. She smiled and, creeping forward, found she had come to the very edge of the forest, with the great River Melde, golden with sunlight, stretched out in front of her. But water wasn't all she saw; sitting on the grass with his back to her was a man, his body silhouetted against the River's brightness, and a long wooden flute tucked to his lips.

She drew back, startled. Her every sense tingled with alarm; the man could be an enemy, a spy, one of her father's soldiers. And yet, as she watched the outline of his form, a strange sensation spread through her veins.

There was something familiar about him and about his music, too. It sounded then very like the haunting melodies she had heard the Ductae play in that time before. She emerged slowly from the woods and the man, suddenly sensing her presence, lowered the flute from his lips and turned to face her.

The instrument slipped, forgotten, from his hands. She looked back at him, trembling.

"Oh, Sweet Maker," breathed Cam. "Paragrin!"

"I don't believe it," she said. "How can you be here?"

"Don't be angry," he begged, rising to his feet, "I couldn't stay away. All that talk about battles being more important than love, well, the more I thought about it, the stupider it seemed. Kerk said I was wrong all along, but I just didn't listen. Paragrin! The whole idea of the Oval and the Rectangle, it's men and women being together, isn't it?"

She stared at him, dumbstruck, and Cam took her hands into his. "You *can* wear the Oval and care for someone, I know you can," he said, "and I can dare to love my Ruler"—he went to his knees before her— "and still not rob her of that dignity."

She pressed his hands.

"In fact," said Cam, heartened by the look in her eyes, "by not loving, you're *denying* the Maker. And remember what you said to Zessiper: 'My duty as a ruler is to follow the Maker's plan.' I heard you say it. It must be true!"

Paragrin gazed at him and smiled. "Then rise, rot you," she whispered, "and kiss me."

Cam stood, and touched her gently on the cheek.

161

"Not there," said Paragrin, and reached up and clasped him about the neck.

Cam looked at her, uncertain, then he bent down and kissed her on the lips—timidly, at first, but then, as his courage grew, passionately; and all of Paragrin's fears fell away at that moment, and she felt stronger, then, than she had ever felt before.

In the morning, they traveled together up the riverbank, and with a log between them, pushed their way across the water. After concealing the Amulet once more beneath her blouse, Paragrin took Cam's hand and walked beside him into Lexterre.

PART THREE

28

They came to the end of the path and stopped, watching as the people of Lexterre bustled back and forth in front of them; women and children carrying buckets of water from the well, and men readying their wooden ploughs for farming.

"It looks so peaceful; as if we'd never left," said Cam, a little disappointed.

"Give it time. Now let's see if we can make it to my—to Strap's—house, before anyone notices us," said Paragrin.

But it was not to be.

"Oh, Dear Father!" came a voice. Halfway across the square, two broad hands seized Cam and spun him about. "My Maker, it *is* you!"

"Yes, hello, Nob," he said, looking helplessly at Paragrin. "How are you?"

165

"Why, I think I should ask *you* that. We all thought you were dead! What are you doing strolling in here without telling a person? Where on this Good Earth have you been? In the River, from the feel of you."

"Well," Cam began.

"Not now," said Paragrin, pulling at his sleeve. "We have to see Strap."

"Oh, I don't believe it," breathed Nob. "Is that little Paragrin?"

She shot him a black look, and Cam stepped in front of her quickly, pushing her toward the house. "Yes, Paragrin's here, too," he said, "though I think you'll find her not as—as 'little' as before."

"Where's your cap, girl?" Nob demanded. "Are those trousers you're wearing?"

"I knew it would be like this," she muttered.

"Forget it. Just keep walking, and we can get to Strap before—"

"Ho, everyone!" Nob yelled. "Cam's come back!"

Suddenly, all action stopped in the square. Every head turned, and in the next second, ploughs, buckets, and children were all abandoned. Everyone crowded up around Cam, asking excitedly where he'd been, what he'd done, and where in the land his brother was. He stood captive in the center of it all, and tried very hard to answer everybody at once. Paragrin, meanwhile, found she went mostly unrecognized, and was just as happy to stay that way, until she overheard two young girls talking behind her.

"Did you see that one up close?" said the first one. "I knew her right away."

"Her?" said the second. "But it has trousers."

"I know," said the first. "It's Paragrin."

"Paragrin! Oh, and she was *banished*."

"I know," said the first. "That's why she's in disguise now. She thinks no one will see her."

Paragrin turned and glared at them—to their great surprise—then made her way through the crowd to Cam. "I'm going now," she said.

"Yes, I'm coming," he answered, but before he left his attentive audience, he put his arm about her waist. "I'm not the only one who's returned," he said with a smile, "so has Paragrin."

"Paragrin!" and all those who hadn't seen, stared out at her in amazement. The crowd hushed, whispers flew about, and several old women shook their heads in scorn.

"Is Strap in his house, Nob?"

"Yes, go on ahead!"

And as the travelers turned and finished their walk across the square, everyone else turned and followed at a safe distance. The novelty of Cam had already died in the reintroduction of Paragrin—who had become somewhat of a legend in Lexterre as the only person brash enough to have been expelled. Some people secretly admired her for it, and now they were set to view the next delicious confrontation—and probable reexpulsion—that was about to take place between brother and sister. They waited, breathless, while Paragrin rapped boldly on the door and stepped back to stand with Cam.

Two hundred eyes watched the door open; Strap was not slow to answer it, and when he saw all the people

167

gathered before him, he stared back at them, wondering—until his gaze fell upon Cam.

"Dear Essai," he breathed, "where have you been?" and he clasped him firmly about the shoulders. "Are you all right?"

"Yes, thank you," said Cam. "I'm fine . . . and so is Paragrin."

"Paragrin . . . ?" And as Cam turned and the crowd turned to see her again, so did Strap. She was waiting for him.

"I've come back," she said.

". . . So I see," said Strap, and there was silence, until a shrill voice rang out behind him.

"Who's there at the door?" it said, and Aridda's face loomed up in the entranceway. She took one look at Paragrin, and dropped her jaw. "Well," she said, "look who's here. You were banished once, does Strap have to do it all over again?"

The crowd stirred, eager.

"I have things I need to say to him," said Paragrin.

"Nothing he needs to hear, I'm sure," Aridda returned.

"Quiet. I won't have our arguments forced on half the town," said Strap. "If you have something new to say to me, Paragrin, you're welcome to enter. Are you with her, Cam?"

"Very much," said the young man, and he took her hand.

"All right then, come in, both of you. I have some questions of my own to ask."

As the travelers passed into the house, Strap turned

to his people. "You can go back to your work now, all of you," he said. "The excitement's over." And he pushed the door shut behind him.

"I bet it's just starting," said the first girl, and the second one, nodding, agreed.

Strap took a seat at the table that stood by the fire, and motioned his sister and Cam to join him; they did, while Aridda examined every inch of Paragrin with disapproval, from her unruly tumble of hair to the fine, strangely familiar boots—their wet black fur glistening in the candlelight.

"Oh, my Father!" she gasped, pointing to Paragrin's feet. "Strap! Those are the bearskin boots I made for you last year!"

"Yes," said Paragrin, "and they've been just wonderful, Aridda, thank you."

Strap held up his hand. "It's not important," he said to his mate. "Now why don't you lend our friends some blankets before they flood us with their dripping, and fill two bowls with some stew. They look as if they haven't eaten in a few days."

"We haven't, much," said Cam, "thank you."

Aridda went off frowning, and Strap turned in his chair to look at the young man. "Where is your brother?" he asked, folding his arms in front of him. "Was Kerk not so lucky to survive your little adventure?"

"Oh, no, he's quite well, thank you. He's just at the Colony."

"The Colony," Strap repeated. "Has he forgotten his duty to this town?"

169

Cam started to answer, but then thought better of it.

"And you," Strap continued, leaning forward, "did you think it was right for you to desert your responsibilities? I might expect that from Kerk, but I always thought you were more trustworthy. We assumed that you had been killed, or taken prisoner at the Melde. On the one hand, I'm delighted to have you back safe; on the other, I'm disgusted that you could have been so thoughtless."

Cam listened quietly to this reproach, and Paragrin, seeing that he was not going to speak quickly in his own defense, spoke for him.

"It was never Cam's intention to stay away," she said. "It's my fault he did."

"It's no one's 'fault,'" said Cam.

"Well, it doesn't surprise me," said Aridda, dropping the bowls in front of the companions. "I always assumed you were at the bottom of the boys' disappearance. Here's the blanket. I can only spare one."

"I went with her willingly always," said Cam, rising to drape it across Paragrin's shoulders. "She's worth everything to me"—and he met Aridda's astonished eyes with a smile. Strap looked from Paragrin to Cam and back again, silent.

"A strange thing happened the night we were in the Melde," Paragrin continued, staring back at him. "I met up with Trag, and he called me by another name: Tempira."

Strap's eyes widened, almost imperceptably, but Paragrin looked for the change, and saw it.

"That *was* strange," said Strap, leaning back in his chair. "So you've stayed in the Melde all this time. Did you live freely, or as prisoners?"

"We left the Colony that night," said Cam.

"But where have you been since then?"

"In a cave," said Paragrin, "many days from here, and on the other side of the River."

"You spent the winter in a cave?"

"Not alone, I hope," said Aridda, narrowing her eyes.

"No, not alone," said Paragrin. "There were over sixty women who lived there, too. They had an entire community within its tunnels and chambers. Apparently it had been their home ever since Trag destroyed the women's settlement, years ago. They were the few who escaped his soldiers." She studied her brother's face. "Do you remember any of this?"

"Well, I remember the raid," said Strap. "I was only a boy at the time, but I recall the day Trag came back with the women."

"It's odd you never told me that they once lived apart from the men," said Paragrin.

"Well, it wasn't really necessary, was it?" said Strap. "Everyone was reunited in the end."

"But obviously not every woman was accounted for," said Paragrin.

"Every important woman was," said Strap after a moment. He rose and took a mug from the mantel, filling it with ale.

"I wonder," said Paragrin, "if there isn't at least one of those 'unimportant' women whose name might sound familiar to you."

171

Strap's fingers tightened around his mug. "Such as?"

"Zessiper," said Paragrin, and the mug slipped and shattered on the floor.

"I *knew* it!" she cried, rising from her stool. "You've known all along about Zessiper and the women's share in the rule! About *my* right to rule! Why didn't you ever tell me?"

"Don't you yell at your brother," Aridda snapped, alarmed herself at Strap's reaction. "I won't have women talking over men in this house!"

"My good woman," said Cam, rising, "*I'd* like to hear his answer, too."

She stared at him, surprised, but was effectively silenced, and, yanking a rag from a hook beside the fireplace, bent down at Strap's feet to wipe up the ale and broken crockery.

Paragrin, her face flushed, glared back at her brother, every inch of her body stinging with fury. Cam stood by, his green eyes fixed quietly on Strap. The man himself stepped out from the wreckage and took his seat again by the table. "I never really knew anything for certain," he began in a small voice. "I mean, it happened so long ago, in Ram's time. It hardly seemed important."

"Hardly seemed important?" Paragrin seethed.

"There hasn't been a woman in command in my lifetime," said Strap, "certainly not in yours. The time for double rule has passed. Zessiper's mad if she still clings to that old principle. I'm sorry you even found out about it. I knew it would only upset you."

"I can't believe what a hypocrite you are," said Paragrin. "All these years you've condemned Trag for deny-

172

ing you your turn to wear the Rectangle, while all along you've denied me my history."

"That's just what it is, your history!" Strap exclaimed. "Women can't rule anymore, Paragrin, don't you understand? People may have believed it was good once, but our grandfather and father came to realize the Maker's true will."

"And what will is that?" demanded Paragrin.

"That men alone should lead; that the Rectangle is superior to the Oval when it comes to governing others."

"You disagree with your father on most things," said Cam. "Why did you believe him in that?"

"Because the confirmation was there, from the Center," Strap returned, pointing to the ground. "Essai saw the foolishness of women's rule, and took their power from them. The Oval Amulet has been gone and destroyed for forty years! The Rectangle remains in the Melde, strong with the Maker's glory. That's all the proof I need."

"Then you're more a fool than Trag," said Paragrin. "He at least knows when he's betraying the Maker. You're too pleased with your own lofty position to notice. Rot you, Strap, it was never Essai's plan to take the Oval; it was *Ram's*. He drove it from the Colony, and Trag wants to destroy it, but all along it's been kept safe from their hands, first with Zessiper, then with my mother Tempira, and then with me after she gave it to me in the Melde ten years ago." She smiled grimly. "The funny part is that it was *here*, in your house, ever since."

Strap looked at her. "I don't believe it," he said. "All

173

this is sacrilege! You talk as you always have, against the Divine Father. I welcomed you, Paragrin, but I see you haven't changed. Get out now, both of you."

"What will it take to convince you of my truth?" Paragrin said, her hand braced on the chain. Cam saw her ready, and turned away.

Strap smiled. "What else? Prove your blasphemous words. Give me the Oval of the Maker's blessing!"

"Here it is, then," said Paragrin, and drawing the iron from around her neck, dropped it on his waiting palm.

There was silence. Strap stared at the Oval, horrified. Aridda got slowly to her feet, the broken crockery still in her hand.

"Leave this house, Paragrin," she breathed, seeing the fear on Strap's face. "You bring nothing but trouble."

"I won't," said the girl, "and you can't tell me what to do. I'm your Ruler, now, and not even Strap can deny it. Can you?" she challenged, turning on him.

"Go away!" cried Aridda, and she lunged at Paragrin, the jagged crockery held out like blades.

Cam sprang forward and caught Aridda's arm; but Strap saw nothing of their struggle. His eyes, once wide with fear, were shut now, squeezed as tightly as the iron in his hand.

"Oh, Dear Father!" he wailed, and fell to his knees.

29

"Oh, but I can't even call It that anymore, can I?" Strap moaned, his fingers spread against the ground. "The Maker won't be a 'Father' at all, if the Oval still lives."

Aridda pulled from Cam and went to her mate, wrapping her arms about his shoulders. "Don't listen to them," she urged. "It's lies, all of it."

"The Oval's no lie," said Strap faintly.

"But this one must be counterfeit!"

He shook his head. "I can feel the Maker in the iron. I held the Rectangle—once—when Trag showed me what I would never own. I felt the same force then. It's real."

"You don't have to sound so disappointed," said Paragrin.

The color rose in Strap's pale face, and he got to

his feet. Paragrin might have shot him a triumphant smile then, if the despair in his eyes hadn't been so obvious. She was silent.

"Here, take it," he hissed, pressing the Amulet to her palm, "and say what you came to say."

"It's been said," she replied, and slipped the iron back around her neck.

"What about the insults?" Strap returned. "The gloating speech, all to do with your brother's stupidity in believing his family?"

She said nothing.

"Why didn't *you* believe?" he demanded. "All along, you went against the lies."

"The lies were bad for me," she answered.

"And for me they were good?" Strap cried. "To realize now, after almost thirty years, that I've been a fool, and a disgrace to my Maker's plan? Do you imagine this feels good? Sweet Divine, my village, everything I've worked for, is *built* on those lies."

"You never meant to go against Essai," said Aridda.

"Everything's going to change!" he wailed.

"Strap . . ." Cam reached out to steady his trembling hands. "Life will just be returning to the way it was, in the better days before Ram and your father ruled."

Strap turned and looked at him as if he believed in the good words the boy was saying; then all at once a new black thought crossed his mind.

"You'll go and rule with him now, won't you?" he charged his sister. "With Trag?"

"He doesn't want me beside him," she returned. "He has no piety in him. He'll do all he can to stop the Oval."

176

Strap considered this. "He'll try to destroy it," he murmured.

"Let him!" cried Aridda.

Paragrin scowled, but Strap took his mate's hand and held it. "We can't, love," he said quietly, "though it might seem a good thing, at first. Yet the Amulet is blessed, and we can't let it be harmed while it's in our care. We are its guardians, for now."

"I'm glad you see that," said Paragrin, "because your dedication is going to be put to the test."

Strap looked at her.

"Trag's coming for the Oval," she concluded, "soon."

"Here?" he breathed.

She nodded.

"You're bringing him to destroy me!" Strap cried, flushed again. "Rot you, this is all your plan, isn't it? Your revenge! Forcing me to risk my town, my life, for *you*."

"Not for me," Paragrin shot back, "for the Oval, for the old ways!"

"Even if she had never returned, Trag would still have come looking," said Cam. "She came to protect the town."

"She never cared for the town, or the people," Strap retorted.

"They're *my* people, now," said the Ruler, "and I care."

Strap stared at her, silenced.

"Now there is a hope," she continued. "The women from the cave are well practiced in warfare, and they're already on their way to help us in our fight against Trag."

"Women?" gasped Aridda.

"Warriors," Cam amended, "and good ones. They know a special way of fighting that surpasses anything Trag's taught his soldiers. With them beside us, we can easily outnumber his army."

"Numbers mean nothing when you talk of women," Strap exclaimed. "Sweet Maker, is this our only salvation?"

"You don't know what you're saying," Paragrin returned, a little hotly. "They're not like ordinary women."

"I don't care if they wear wolf tails and carry spears," Strap said, "they can't defend my village! Why am I being punished? I never meant to be impious, surely the Maker knows that. I broke from the Melde to be able to serve It better. Lexterre's a vast improvement, despite what mistakes I have unwittingly made. I always believed I was doing right!"

"Strap, you have to trust us," said Cam. "Lexterre can survive with their help."

"There's a lot more at stake than your precious town anyway," snapped Paragrin, "though you're too full of self-pity now to see it."

"I know what's at stake!"

"Then accept what I say, and let me get on with my work. You're not the only one I have to convince, there's a whole village to explain things to."

"To take command over," he said.

She looked at him, steadily. "For now, yes."

"Strap! You can't let her disgrace you like this!" Aridda cried. "She's only a girl. She can't command."

"I wear the Oval, and I *do* command," said Paragrin,

"whether I have his approval or not."

"Then go ahead," said Strap, in a quiet voice. "Go ahead without me, and see if this town will hear a word you say."

"Now listen," Cam said, "the two of you have to appear as a team, or the whole meaning of the Oval and the Rectangle will be lost on them."

"Strap's never worn the Rectangle," said Paragrin, "and I can do very well without him." And turning on her heel, she strode through the door and into the square.

30

Paragrin moved through the busy square as a ruler would—proudly—and all the people turned from their work to stare at her as she stepped up onto the leader's stage. Without a second thought, she took the calling sticks in hand and beat them against the drum. The familiar boom sounded through the village and out over the fields, and any who hadn't been in the square already, came.

"What is this?" demanded a man who had come, hoe in hand, from his work. "Where's Strap?"

From the platform Paragrin could see her brother standing outside the house, his arms crossed defiantly in front of him. "Where he is, is unimportant," she announced, "for he wears no iron of rulership. I have come in this time of trouble to lead you toward a better, more natural way of living."

The people looked to each other, wondering.

"The only trouble we have is you," said Nob, and he was answered by a number of cheers. "Get off the stage, Paragrin, before I knock you off."

"Strap, why are you letting this happen?" Cam said, seizing his arm. "If you went up there with her, all this could be avoided."

"She wanted independence, let her try a taste of it," he replied.

"Why can't you look beyond your anger for a moment?" Cam implored. "This is no petty rivalry anymore, this is a struggle to return the Maker's plan. Why are you standing in Its way?"

Strap met his gaze, but said nothing, and Cam, exasperated, left him.

"Listen to me," said Paragrin, holding her iron high, "because I wear the sacred Oval Amulet and I am made your true leader by Essai. Some may not know the iron's form, but many of you, like Strap, know its history."

"Essai took the real Oval and destroyed it!" a woman exclaimed.

"No! But Trag wants you to believe that," the Ruler returned. "And he's coming to this town to take the Oval himself and keep the truth from his people."

The mention of Trag brought a hush over most of the crowd, but Nob was unimpressed by the warning. "She's just as mad as she ever was," he proclaimed, "and I'm not going to hear her tales."

"They're not tales!" said Paragrin. "Listen to me. I wear the Oval!"

"Give me that," said Nob, and leaping up on the platform, he reached for the iron.

In that dangerous moment, a newly acquired instinct took over. Before she knew what she was doing, Paragrin stepped forward, grabbed Nob's arm, and flipped him off the stage to the ground. The crowd drew back with a gasp, but no one was as surprised as she was.

"I—I'm sorry," she said, as much to the crowd as to Nob. "I don't want to fight. All I want is for you to listen to what I say!"

"Are we going to take this outrage?" demanded the man in front, throwing down his hoe.

"Listen to her!" Cam urged, breaking through to the stage. "She's telling the truth. Trag *is* coming!"

"You're as mad as she is," sputtered Nob, getting to his feet. "No right woman can do what she did!"

"Throw them out before they affect the children," called a woman, clutching her wide-eyed daughter to her skirts.

"Wait!" cried Cam, but it was too late. Six young men, more eager than righteous, sprang from the crowd to seize the rebels. Cam was too stunned by their unthinking response to resist, and though Paragrin flipped two more to the ground, she was soon as well governed as he.

"To the River!" cried a man, as the crowd fell in around them.

"Get the Oval first," Nob shouted.

Paragrin kicked and tried to yell from behind her captor's quieting hand, but Nob reached once more for the iron—and caught it.

"Stop!" came a voice, and Nob's hold on the iron faltered. "Let it go," said the voice, and Nob's hand, like the people's resolution, fell away. "You've no right

182

to touch it," said Strap, pushing Nob aside, "or her. Let her go." His voice was weak, yet still commanding, and the young men grudgingly let her free.

"Cam, too?" asked the other boys sadly, continuing to hold him in their grip.

Paragrin made a move toward them, and the boys, recalling how she had handled their peers, reached a common mind in a glance and released him.

Strap looked at Paragrin and at Cam, putting out a hand to his shoulder; then he walked slowly through the crowd back to the leader's stage. The people watched him in silence, and moved obediently to hear him speak. Strap paused before he mounted the platform.

"I think I've no real right to stand here," he said quietly, "for I've led you wrong. Not on purpose; never on purpose; I've been as deluded as you, but I—I should have known . . . somehow . . . that it was wrong."

Paragrin stood at the back of the crowd, following his every word. Cam glanced at her.

"Everything my sister said was right," he continued. "The Oval she wears is the real one—I've held it—and so it follows that what we learned from Trag and Ram about the women's rule being stopped is false. Essai is in that iron; Essai—not the Father, but the *Mother*, too— means to have the rightful woman lead us. Paragrin is rightful, not only through Trag, but also through her mother. She is daughter to Tempira and granddaughter to Zessiper. She is . . . chosen."

The people looked from Strap to each other and back to Paragrin, amazed. The young Ruler said nothing, but waited for her brother to finish.

"My sister also says that Trag has learned of the Oval's

183

reappearance and is coming here to reclaim it," he said. "The Amulet is blessed, and we must all try to protect it, though he'll be coming with his soldiers, and—and there will be no way to save it. We must all probably die in the attempt, and Lexterre will be taken and— and . . ."

"Things are not as bleak as my brother paints them," said Paragrin, suddenly moving through the disheartened crowd. She stepped onto the stage again beside him, and though he started to leave, she touched his arm and, with a look, asked him to stay. "There are warriors coming to help us."

The people brightened, but Aridda had her say. "They're women," she announced, "not warriors!"

"They're women *and* warriors," Paragrin returned.

"You all saw what she was able to do with Nob and the others," said Cam, coming to stand beside the stage. "That's just a sample of what these warriors can do."

"And most important, they're all of them determined to defeat Trag," said Paragrin, "and return the land to its natural, healthy beginning, with two people, a woman *and* a man," she said, reaching for her brother, "ruling together." Strap looked at her, uncertain, but Cam, seeing their reunion, smiled.

"But what will this mean to women?" demanded a mother. "Will we be expected to fight, in this new rule? To abandon our families?"

"Will there still be Joinings?" asked another.

"She'll want us to become like her," cried Aridda, "capless and rough."

Paragrin colored, but drove the anger to her hands,

184

which clenched, rather than to her voice. "Of course there will be Joinings," she said. "What the double rule offers, finally, is a choice among many ways of life, not just one. Some women may choose to serve as warriors, but certainly you all aren't expected to; others may serve as weavers or farmers. Men may want to cook, and no longer will others think of it," she added, smiling at Cam, "as peculiar."

"It's too different!" said the man with the hoe. "It will never work."

"It *has* worked for centuries," said Paragrin. "What Lexterre does now is 'different.' We are merely returning to the life the Maker intended us to have."

Strap lowered his eyes and, after a moment, he stepped quietly from the stage.

"Everyone here has already pledged themselves to Essai," she continued. "Now the test of dedication has come. You, out of all the people of the land, have been chosen to witness the final confrontation between the evil that Trag has spread and the piety of the old ways. What will take place in this town will be the most important thing you do in your lifetime."

The crowd was silent, every face lifted to the woman on the platform, listening.

"It may be that we are defeated," said Paragrin, "but with all my heart, I do not think that that will happen. I believe, with the warriors and the Maker's trust on our side, that we *will* succeed, and go on to live good and better lives."

Strap walked slowly past the people to his house.

"I realize," said Paragrin, "that I haven't always

185

treated you or this town with much respect, but that time is gone. I am honored now to be your Ruler, and I am honored to be able to lead you in this return to the old ways. Will you rally behind me to put an end, finally, to Trag's tyranny? Do I, and this sacred Oval, have your dedication?"

And as Strap gently closed the door behind him, he could hear his people, cheering.

31

A moment ago, the sun had set behind the forest, and the sky was burning like the fires the Ductae had built about their campsite. Huddled near the flames on the cool spring night, the women took their meal and wondered what would happen in the days ahead. The prospect of battle in a strange land had lost some of its glamor after Paragrin left, and it had taken much of Atanelle's strength to bring them, as committed again, from the cave. Her original warriors, of course, were helps to her, but the person from whom she had expected the most support gave the least. In fact, Atanelle suspected the troop's new uneasiness stemmed mostly from this unhelpful behavior.

"She's just not herself, anymore," said the warrior, as she took a walk that night with Jentessa. "I can't understand it. What happened to that Glorious Ruler I knew as a girl, that level-headed woman I tried to imitate? Why, she moves so queerly now; and did you hear the way she complained when we decided to stop? After a whole day of traveling!"

"She is anxious for battle," said Jentessa.

"Well, so am I, but not like that. I mean, we have to arrive in good health, don't we? There are older women among us; I have to look out for them."

Jentessa nodded. "It's just hard for Zessiper to see that. She's older than anyone."

"I know," said the warrior, "and that's why it's even more peculiar. She has all our energy!"

Jentessa stopped to rest then in a clearing, and fell silent, staring up at the stars that were beginning, now, to appear. "We must all be patient with her," she said at last, in a quiet voice. "She has lived such a troubled life, sacrificed much, suffered much." Jentessa frowned. "The world has been unfair to her. If she is, in the end, a little unfair to the world, so be it."

The warrior looked at Jentessa, wondering at the defiance in her voice, but the Holy Intermediator said nothing more, and at length Atanelle gazed up at the stars herself. There was peace then for a time, until suddenly a sound came from the brush behind them. They turned, and saw Zessiper—her face and hands lifted up to the night—wandering among the trees, laughing.

32

Far from the Ductae, on the other side of the River, Cam and Paragrin sat by the water and talked. This was their first time alone together all that eventful day, and they took good advantage of the peace that the night afforded them.

"I'm proud of you," said Cam, putting his arm around her waist. "That was no easy feat to convince the villagers. I even think Nob's going to trust you."

"Well, it certainly started off wrong," she agreed, settling into his hold, "but I'm pleased how everything ended. These people aren't as bad as I thought. I really think they're going to help us."

Suddenly there came a voice. "Cam!"

The two of them jumped and turned about. Ellagette was standing apart from them, back by the path.

189

"Come here, Cam," she said, "I want to talk to you."

The companions exchanged a glance, then he rose and went to her.

"Hello, Ellagette," he said, "how are—"

"What happened to Kerk?" she demanded. "There's much talk, but I can't get the same story twice. Why didn't he come back with you? Is he really all right, or is he hurt—or worse?"

"Oh, no," Cam assured her. "He's . . . well, he just didn't want to come back yet. He's at the Melde."

"Doing what?"

He shot a desperate look to Paragrin. "Oh, I don't know," Cam said at last. "Helping with the planting, maybe."

Ellagette gave a snort of disgust and tossed her head. Her eyes sparkled in the moonlight, and Paragrin thought again how pretty she was.

"I shouldn't have asked," said the girl. "I can well imagine what he's doing." She paused. "Is he coming back for this battle?"

"No," said Cam, "I don't think so."

"I don't think so, either," she returned. "He never was one for causes, was he? Well," she said, glancing down at Paragrin, "don't let me disturb you, Cam." She started for the path, then stopped, and after a moment of debate, turned and bowed her head to the Ruler before hurrying away.

"What do you think of that?" said Paragrin. "First Nob shows respect, now Ellagette!"

"You'd better get used to it," Cam laughed, coming to sit again beside her. "They'll all be looking to you now."

190

"Well, we'll be all right," said Paragrin. "I'll get them to review their weapon use tomorrow, and I've already assigned two people to keep watch tonight. Everything will work out." She sighed. "I suppose we should be getting back. It's late."

"Aridda banished me from your house until morning," said Cam. "Of course, I wasn't even going to *suggest* that I stay."

"Weren't you?" said Paragrin, leaning toward him.

"Not in this town," he returned. "At least, not until we can be . . . can be . . ."

Paragrin stiffened, her eyes suddenly fixed on the water.

"That is," he faltered, and fell silent, poking at the earth with his fingers.

A moment passed.

"Cam," asked Paragrin quietly, "will you become Joined with me?"

He looked at her, surprised, then nodded. "Oh, *yes!*"

"Then let's not go back quite yet," she said softly, her eyes shining in the night. "Let's give Aridda something to scold about," and she lay back against the grass.

Cam looked down at her, and smiled.

Back at the house, Strap sat on his bed, mute, the pale light from the moon striking his face. Aridda sat for a time in silence beside him; then she rose, and pulled the cloth across the window.

"I love you," she whispered, and knelt down before him.

For a second, he did nothing; then, with a gasp, he turned his head to her breast, and wept.

In the morning, when Cam was allowed back inside again, the companions sat with Strap at the table to make plans over breakfast.

"These are wonderful," said Cam, taking his second biscuit from the plate. "I'd like you to show me how to make them, sometime."

Aridda paused in her sewing to stare at him.

"So the watchers saw nothing? I expected as much," said Paragrin. "The Ductae shouldn't come until tomorrow."

"What about Trag?"

"You don't need to worry, Strap. He won't come until after the women."

"How do you know? Did he give you his word?"

Paragrin smiled. "It will all work out."

"I need more assurance than that," Strap demanded. "I can't sit here idle all day, while Lexterre is in danger."

"You won't be idle. We're going to train the people to use their weapons in battle. You can make certain everyone has a spear—the women, too."

"That's not enough!" said Strap. "I want something for the land itself. A—a wall, or something."

"That's ridiculous," said Paragrin. "What good could a wall do?"

"Keep Trag out, for one."

"A wall we made couldn't keep him out. And what would we make it from? Chairs? Tables?"

"If we had to, yes!" cried Strap.

"Paragrin, maybe a wall just around the *square* wouldn't be bad," said Cam, kicking her gently with his foot. "If Strap thinks it would help, then maybe it would."

She frowned. "Oh, all right. Go ahead and do your wall, for all the good it will serve. But they'll still have to ready their weapons."

Strap rose from his chair to put on his boots.

"I'll come with you," said Cam. He stuffed a biscuit in his pocket, and followed Strap out the door.

Paragrin sat alone at the table, chewing her food resentfully. She glanced about the room, and was surprised, suddenly, to see Aridda. The woman had been so quiet during their breakfast that she had forgotten she was even there. But now Aridda looked across at her with such blatant hostility that Paragrin stopped her chewing. She frowned again and, pushing aside her plate, rose and went out, slamming the door behind her.

All day the ploughs stood abandoned in the fields as the people of Lexterre made ready for battle. Paragrin was pleased to see them unite so well, and even agreed, after a sturdy wall of mud and wood had been built, that it might prove a help to them after all.

"Who knows?" she said. "At least it might stall him, and that could be useful. We can even have our weapons inside and strike the soldiers down when they climb into it."

"When did you say your 'warriors' would come?" asked Strap.

"They'll be in time, don't worry. Together, we'll defeat Trag, and," she added cheerfully, "you'll finally get to wear the Rectangle."

Strap turned his back. "I don't even want it anymore," he said bitterly, and walked off.

193

"Rot him, anyway," Paragrin said. "He's been no good since this whole thing began. Great Maker, Cam, you've been more of a leader than *he* has."

"This must be very hard on him," said Cam, watching him disappear again into his house.

"Look at these people," Paragrin snapped, pointing to the weary villagers who stood about in the square. "It's hard on everyone," and she went to inspect the arrows.

By dusk, Lexterre had grown nervous. Arguments erupted over nothing. Fist fights broke out twice, and a false alarm sent one man to bed with an arrow wound in his side. Even Cam lashed out at Strap over his handling of the people, and though he apologized the next moment, he couldn't quite quell the growing tension within him.

"How can you be so certain that the women will get here before Trag?" he asked Paragrin, as they stood that night at the watch.

"It's because of Jentessa," she said. "She wouldn't let it happen."

"How could she stop it?"

"I don't know," said Paragrin. "She just seems to *do* things. You know."

"Yes," said Cam, then added, "but maybe he's supposed to come first."

She looked at him sharply. "What do you mean?"

"Well," said Cam, "Jentessa has 'let' other bad things occur. Maybe this time will be another."

Paragrin turned away. "I don't believe that will happen," she said.

194

And at morning, the village was still safe, and Paragrin prepared herself to welcome the Ductae. But just as the sun began to climb in the sky, two scouts came running back from the River, breathless. They had seen him. They had seen him. Trag and his army were here.

33

"Oh, my Maker, I knew this would happen!" cried Strap.

Paragrin stood alone, so stunned by the news that she said nothing.

"What are you going to do?" Strap demanded, seizing her by the jacket. "Where are your precious Ductae now, to save us?"

"Get inside the wall with the fighters," said Paragrin, in a voice so tight that Cam could barely recognize it as hers. "Everyone else should abandon their homes and hide by the far fields. Tell them," she said, turning to Cam, and he was off.

By the time he returned, and climbed into the square, Cam could hear the drum of the soldiers' feet as they marched up from the River. He ran to the part of the wall that faced the path and crouched down beside Strap and Paragrin.

"Everyone's hidden," he whispered. "Aridda wanted to come, but I told her the people would need her more there. She stayed."

". . . Thank you," said Strap.

Cam leaned back on the wall, catching his breath, and looked at Paragrin. Never had he seen her face so drawn. "It'll be all right," he said, taking her hand, "somehow." Paragrin shot him an unconvincing smile. "What do we do now?" he asked.

"We stall him," she replied, "for as long as we're able."

Suddenly the marching stopped, and there came a silence, a silence so thick that everyone within the wall fell silent too, and listened. For another moment, nothing; then the slow and heavy footsteps of a man—a large man—sounded against the earth, growing louder, louder, as they approached the wall. Then there was silence again, until—

"Well. This is unexpected."

The tone of his father's voice—so blissfully forgotten—invaded Strap's senses again like a sickness. It had been ten years since he had heard it last, but time collapsed around him now, and he shrank back against the wall, breathless.

"There seems to be no one here," said Trag. His boots sounded again on the earth, back and forth in front of the wall. Paragrin's hand moved to the blade at her belt. "If there's no one here," Trag continued, "then it wouldn't matter if we pulled apart these little houses."

"Go away, rot you!" Strap cried.

Paragrin jumped at the sudden shout, but Trag,

at the other side of the wall, smiled.

"So, my son," he said, "how fine to hear you again. I only wish I could *see* you. What is this ridiculous barrier? You must have known I was coming, and imagined this could keep me and my soldiers out. But Strap, I have no argument with you—except for the old one—*and* that you've kept the other Amulet hidden from me all these years. Tell me, what use did you think it would serve you, boy? You can't wear *that* one"—and Trag smiled at the flush he knew he had caused. "But all is forgiven," he continued. "I and my soldiers will spare your town, *if* you send over the girl—with the Oval, of course."

Paragrin glanced at her brother.

"Think of it, my buck!" said Trag.

Strap did think of it, and seeing his longing, Cam made ready to spring to Paragrin's defense; but Strap closed tight his eyes, as if suddenly in pain, and struck the ground with his fist. *"You lied to me!"* he shouted, in a voice heard far in the fields.

"I what?"

"You lied to me!" Strap cried, grabbing the wall as if it were he. "Everything about the Oval being taken, destroyed by Essai. I built my whole life on that principle, that men alone should rule!"

"It never did you any harm," came the voice.

"You don't know harm!" Strap wailed. "Essai was never in your heart. May the Maker forgive me for my blasphemies!"

"Enough of this touching confession," said Trag irritably. "Give me your sister, and it will all be done with."

198

Strap reached out for her, and Paragrin would have drawn her knife then and there, if she hadn't felt the tear that fell to her hand when he touched it.

"I won't," said Strap. "At least now I can show my true faith. The Oval was meant to rule beside the man, and I'll honor the sacred plan to the end."

"Then the end it will be," said Trag flatly. "Joel, Klay," he called to his men, "set fire to the village."

"No!" Strap cried, and tearing the knife from Paragrin's belt, he jumped to his feet and over the wall. Trag stumbled backward, surprised, and put out his hand to defend himself. He deflected the blade from his heart, but surrendered his arm as the sharp edge slashed across his skin. He howled, and seizing Strap with one large hand, he drew his own knife from its sheath and thrust it forward. Strap shrieked, and his blade, stained with his father's blood, fell from his grip. He collapsed; Trag caught him for a moment in his arms, and the great Ruler stared down at his son as if not yet believing what had happened. Then, with a shudder, he released him, and Strap dropped lifeless to the ground.

"Sweet Essai," Cam breathed, peering over the wall. "Trag's killed him."

The news spread like fire through the square. Some of the fighters threw down their weapons; others abandoned their posts in horror.

"Everyone, back to your places!" yelled Paragrin, but Trag's soldiers had already mounted the walls. With an angry shout, she knocked one across the barrier, and tackled another as he fell; but three more came to their rescue, and took her.

199

Cam, fearing for Paragrin's life, rushed at the captors, but a spear shaft struck his shoulders, and he was taken.

Paragrin was pulled, subdued yet defiant, to stand before the others, her Amulet glinting in the morning sun. Trag dragged himself over the wall, swearing as he came, and clutching at his bloody arm, but when he turned and saw the Oval before him, he fell silent. There was a moment, then he raised his eyes slowly to meet hers.

"Oh, my daughter," he whispered, "I've found you now."

34

The wearer of the Rectangle and the wearer of the Oval confronted each other in the square, each saying more with their eyes than their words could possibly have expressed. Then Trag reached out to her face; Paragrin flinched, and he moved instead to the iron.

"Do you know that the last time I saw this I was a boy, and the women were marching from the city in droves?" he murmured. "How fine to have it again."

"You don't have it yet," said Paragrin.

Trag smiled, and took his hand from the Oval, leaving behind his blood glistening on the iron. "Just like your mother," he said. "Joel, give me your scarf. I'm bleeding," and as the soldier relinquished the cloth, Trag took and wrapped it around his arm. "There are people missing," he said, looking about at the captured fighters.

201

"Where's the rest of the village? In hiding?"

Paragrin said nothing.

"Find them," said Trag to his soldiers, "and bring them here."

"They're not important," said Paragrin. "Your quarrel's with me."

"So it is," Trag returned, "but I'll have them, still."

"Should we take her necklace?" asked one of her captors, reaching for the iron.

Trag struck his hand away. "Don't touch it; that Oval is worth more than your life. Give her to me," he said, pulling Paragrin from the soldiers. "We have things to discuss."

"Let her go!" Cam exclaimed, struggling to free himself. "Paragrin, don't let that murderer take you!"

Trag, with Paragrin held firmly in his arm, looked to see who had spoken. When his glare fell on Cam, he frowned. "Another face that I recognize," he said. "We've had words once before, haven't we, boy?" He turned to the men that held Cam prisoner. "Find some strong branches," he said, "and beat him."

"No!" cried Paragrin, clutching at his arm.

Trag looked down at her thoughtfully. "Just hold him, then," he amended, and went out to the houses beyond, pulling his newfound daughter behind him.

He took her to the house at the head of the square, and Paragrin, seeing Strap's things laid about in the room, felt her loathing for Trag sink deeper than it had ever been before. When he released her, she shrank back.

202

"Not frightened, are you?" said Trag. "Tempira was never frightened."

"I'm not scared," said Paragrin, "I'm sickened. Every awful thing you've done is stained in your eyes, from forcing the women from their settlement, to killing my mother. *I hate you*."

"Listen," said Trag, grabbing her wrist, "I don't care what you feel for me, but I do care that you understand. I didn't kill Tempira."

"You raped her!" cried Paragrin.

"That was *her* choice!" Trag returned angrily. "I never wanted to hurt her. I loved her, can't you understand?"

Paragrin pulled again from him, but Trag caught and pinned her against the hearth. "Listen to me," he demanded, "I don't know what rot you've been fed, but Tempira was out to ruin me from the start. All I wanted from her was a family, a mate, and a fine son to receive my Amulet—a boy with the great bloods of both rulers surging in his veins. But for all, she gave nothing, only misery—and a daughter."

"Her successor, not yours," said Paragrin, and smiled.

"You're not a Ruler," said Trag. "You rule over no one. The Oval was taken and destroyed by the Maker, and it will stay destroyed. Now I have no wanting to hurt you, girl; you're her blood, and I would treat you with respect. You can come back to the Melde and live free, with all the privilege that such a daughter deserves. But you must obey my law. You must give me that Oval, and *willingly* relinquish your claim to power."

Paragrin stared at him, her eyes glowing with an old

fire. "Do you really think that I would give over the one treasure my mother was able to keep from your filthy hands?" she breathed. "For eight years, she kept it buried in the earth in the hope that one day she would find a chance in her guarded life to pass it on to me. That child who received it didn't even know what the iron meant! There wasn't even enough time for her to tell me. I, the wearer of the Oval, was unaware of my power and duty to my people for *ten years*. What pain you've caused, Trag! What horrible, lasting pain you and your own father's wretched lies have caused this land. You're a fool if you think I'd give this over to you now," she said, clutching the iron to her chest. "You'll have to kill me to get it."

"Rot you!" cried Trag, and he flung her to the floor, his hand raised again to strike her as she lay, but he stopped, trembling. "No, I won't kill you," he panted, "not again . . . but there are other ways. Mott, Klay!" he shouted, "bring in that boy!"

"No!" screamed Paragrin.

He turned and hauled her to her feet. "Then give me that Amulet of your own will."

Paragrin pulled away, her eyes brimming with tears. "No," she said again.

He scowled, and looked to the men who had brought in the prisoner.

"Paragrin, are you all right?" Cam implored, seeing her tears. "What has he done to you?"

"Nothing yet," Trag answered, and caught hold of Cam's jaw with one large hand. "You see, my buck," he said, "I've just made an offer of fair exchange to my daughter. I give her a life in the Melde, and she gives me that iron. Now this is a more than reasonable trade, and yet she said she was willing to die for it." Trag narrowed his eyes as he looked at her. "Now for reasons of my own, I would rather not have her killed, so the offer has been changed. The question is, my friend, is she willing to let *you* die for it?" and he smiled to see Paragrin's stricken face.

Cam saw it too, and after a moment he took a deep breath and spoke. "I love you, Paragrin," he declared, "but if you give him that Oval after all we've been through, I swear I'll never forgive you."

She stared back at him, shattered, but fiercely proud.

"Great Maker!" Trag thundered. "Do you think I won't do it?" and he seized Cam by the throat, pulling his knife again from its sheath.

"Oh, Essai!" Paragrin whispered, closing her eyes. *"Help us."*

"TRAG!"

A soldier burst in the room, his expression wild. "Trag! You've got to come! There's another army."

Paragrin opened her eyes and looked at him.

"They came upon us all at once! What do you want us to do?"

Trag stared at the soldier, confounded. "What are you talking about?" he demanded. "Are these the hidden villagers?"

"Dear Father, no!" cried the man. "They've got armor, and everything! There are as many of them as there are of us. Trag, we weren't ready for this. What are we going to *do*?"

205

"Quiet!" said Trag, and he turned to Paragrin. "What do you know of it?" he demanded, but she said nothing. "Augh!" he swore, and shoved Cam to the floor. "I'll finish with this later," he promised, and ran out the door with his soldiers in tow.

Paragrin fell to her knees beside Cam and embraced him. He was shaking from the closeness of his murder, and without saying a word, he tucked his face to her blouse and held her.

"Oh, thank the Maker . . ." Paragrin whispered, stroking his hair tenderly to soothe him, "Atanelle, you've come at last."

35

She had seen him. She had not expected to see him. Not here, not yet; but there he was, crouching behind a tree as she and the Ductae stepped quietly—oh, so quietly—through the forest to surprise Trag. But they had surprised *him* first.

Ram, who had thought to remove himself from the grossness of the seige, was enjoying a moment of ease when the second army had suddenly emerged. He started, his short-sightedness revealing only indefinite shapes; but sometimes one can know the shape of a person so well—their walk, their stance, their very smell—that one can recognize it even through a haze, and so he did; for his imperious younger cousin had never really left him—she had haunted his dreams for almost forty years. And now she was here.

Their eyes met, both of them freezing their movement with the unutterable thrill of the moment. Ram paled, his eyes bulged, his jaw fell open; Zessiper's heart jumped, her eyes blazed. A flash of astonishment, and they were off: Ram turning tail and beginning to run as fast as he could, deeper into the forest; a second later, Zessiper leaping after him, her face wild with the glory of the chase.

On and on, deeper into the woods. Ram, smaller, and more used to woods than she, just managing to keep ahead of her; Zessiper, stumbling and falling in her frenzy as she ran, yet rising each time to run again, her face never losing its strange, joyous light, her eyes never off the fleeing figure ahead of her.

And then Ram began to slow, his old heart beating furiously in his chest. She, younger, stronger, and made invincible with passion, came closer, closer. Ram screamed in fear, and fell, tumbling to the ground.

Zessiper cried out and came upon him, her teeth bared in a vicious smile, her spear held tightly in her hand.

Ram screamed again, and curled himself into a ball among the pine needles, his bony fingers waving spastically over his face.

Zessiper panted heavily, catching her breath. She looked down, confused, at the quivering mass at her feet, and something inside of her was slowed. She blinked and looked again. She saw an old man shaking with fright, his pouchy, watery eyes squeezed shut, his arms and legs shriveled, his hair scarce, stringy, his voice shrill. She blinked again, her spear held with less conviction. Ram begged for mercy, and slowly Zessiper let down her spear, a feeling of disappointment and disgust cooling her vengeance. This wasn't the Enemy. This wasn't the terrible foe for whom she had nursed a hatred for forty years. This was only . . . pathetic. Too easy. Much, much too easy.

"I haven't done a thing!" Ram shrieked. "And I had nothing to do with Tempira!"

Zessiper's heart leaped again at the name.

Ram struggled to his knees, his hands trembling as he clenched and unclenched his fists in front of him. "It's not my fault what happened! It's Trag's. It's *Trag's* fault! He killed your daughter!"

Zessiper stiffened. She breathed unevenly, her eyes misting as she saw it again: Tempira, standing up to him, but he striking her down, binding her wrists, carrying her away . . . away. . . .

"TRAG!" Zessiper thundered, her arms stretched out at her sides.

Ram looked up, astounded. He pressed his advantage. "That's right, Cousin, it was Trag. Big Trag! He killed her. And listen . . . he has your granddaughter, now."

Zessiper's eyes widened. She looked down, disbelieving.

"It's true!" said Ram.

"Paragrin . . ." whispered Zessiper, her spear clenched once more in her hand.

"Yes, *Paragrin*," Ram insisted, "and he'll get her, he'll kill her, just like he did Tempira!"

"NO!" Zessiper cried. "No!" and she turned, wild again, and ran back through the forest toward Lexterre.

209

It was Trag. It was him all along. It was—"TRAG!" she bellowed, and disappeared into the distance.

Ram watched her go. "I always knew she was mad," he said.

36

Trag ran back to the square, and with his hand still clenched about his knife, confronted the army that stood now within the walls. He glared at them, trying to find a man that he could recognize, when all at once a broad smile crept across his face. "My Maker," he breathed, "they're women.

"You fools!" he cried, turning to his soldiers, who had backed with their village captives against the wall. "They're only women! Is this what you were afraid of?"

"They've reason to be afraid," said Atanelle, though the soldiers had straightened themselves and pushed their prisoners forward again. "We are the Ductae warriors, and have come, under the glorious command of our Ruler who wears the Oval, to take back what is ours." She glanced about her, suspiciously. "Where *is* our Ruler?" she demanded.

"Here!" exclaimed Paragrin, and rushed to the square.

A light came to the warriors' eyes when they saw their leader at last, and Atanelle took Paragrin's hand and knelt down before her. "We have come again to your service," she proclaimed.

"How touching," said Trag, replacing his knife in its sheath. "Tell me, where did you find these strange people?"

"These," said Paragrin, turning to confront him again, "are the women who escaped your bloody raid eighteen years ago, when you took my mother from their settlement. Many were only children when they saw you last, but everyone remembers."

The women looked at Trag then with such malice, clutching their spears all the while, that some of the soldiers backed away again, holding their prisoners less boldly. Paragrin glanced about for her grandmother and was puzzled not to see her; but other matters took her attention now.

"As you can tell, they have come to defy you," said Paragrin, "and save the Melde from your tyranny."

"How do they propose to do that?" asked Trag.

"Will you continue," she demanded, "to reject the Maker's will?"

"It's your notion that I reject Him," said Trag with a smile, "not mine."

"Then I offer you this solution," said Paragrin. "Your soldiers, at our command, will engage in a hand-to-hand battle with mine, with no weapons being used on either side. Whichever army succeeds in subduing the other will be the victor."

"Do you mean to say," said Trag slowly, "that when my men defeat your women, you'll give me the Oval of your free will, and surrender your claim to power?"

Paragrin's fingers curled around her iron. "Yes," she said, "and when my women defeat your men, you'll give me your Rectangle, and surrender *your* claim."

"What of the villagers?" Trag demanded. "They can't take part in this."

"Agreed," said Paragrin.

"Then I accept your offer. Soldiers, release the prisoners."

"But Paragrin," shouted Nob, "you'll need us!"

"No," said the Ruler. "Stay back. The agreement has been made." She turned to the women. "Are you ready?"

Atanelle laid her spear against the wall and nodded.

"And so," Trag said with a laugh, "let the game begin!"

Then the two armies approached each other slowly across the square like the players in a grand dance—eyes watching eyes, hands poised, feet stepping cautiously over the ground—and then suddenly they converged, and the square turned to a swirl of wolf tails and braids, with Paragrin in the midst of it, eager and strong.

"Cam!"

He turned. "Jentessa!" he cried, and caught the woman in his arms. "I'm so glad to see you! Look, I think we're going to win this battle after all, without bloodshed. Trag doesn't know what he's agreed to. I'm going to go do what I can."

"I think you had better stay," said Jentessa, keeping

his hand; "you might be mistaken for the wrong side."

"Oh," said Cam, stepping back, "I suppose you're right."

"Besides, our Ruler is doing well enough on her own," she said, and they watched Paragrin flip another soldier to the ground.

Trag watched too, as his men, baffled by the women's gymnastics, were being beaten down one by one. He stared amazed as the wolf tails began to disappear from the clump of the fighting, and the braids, swinging into the air as the women swirled about, seemed to grow more numerous.

What was it that was happening? he wondered. What strange, powerful dance was it that the women had within them, that made his men slump against the walls, groaning? It was unreal! It was unnatural. He felt that a force, stronger than any he had known, must be at work now tormenting him, bringing his glory crashing to the ground. Why would it happen? Then a dark thought struck him. What if Strap with his anguished confessions had been right about the Maker's wrath? What if Essai, silent for so many years, had at last decided that the lone Ruler of the Melde would fall?

His breath came quickly. He turned from the fight, and saw them, then: the eyes, clear and sharp as ice, holding him from across the square, filled with the silent judgment of the Center. He spun away chilled from Jentessa's gaze, and again the struggle was before him.

It was worse. The women were winning. Trag breathed hard as he saw his daughter, the Amulet swinging against her chest, bring another soldier to the

214

ground. She was glowing, triumphant; and Trag, clutching his own iron in his fist, began to burn. He would not let it happen. He would never let her take his power! his Amulet . . . not her, not anyone . . . or any*thing*.

He drew his knife again from its sheath, and moving forward, plucked a woman from the fight, dragging her back by her braid. She tried to twist in his grasp to confront him, but he held her tight, pinned against his body, and in one quick move, slid his blade across her throat. She screamed—a queer scream—and was silent.

"This is how you win a battle, rot you!" Trag cried to his men. The brawl in the square stopped—and everyone turned to stare at the body Trag held high above his head, the blood from her wound trickling down his arm. He flung the body forward, and the people pulled away, horrified, as it landed with a thud on the ground.

There was silence. Paragrin's triumphant smile faded. Jentessa's bright eyes went dull. Cam, sickened, turned away.

Then suddenly the silence was broken as Atanelle, with an angry shout, raced toward Trag, her blade drawn. Three of her women joined her, but a company of Trag's men—the older, more willing ones—rose up to defend him. The other fighters stood apart, uncertain. The clash of blade against blade sounded from the skirmish, and cautiously the others brought out their knives. One of the soldiers screamed as he was stabbed by Atanelle, and a younger Colonist from the crowd lashed out in retaliation. Then another fighter joined in, and then another and another. The battle had begun again, and even the righteous townspeople defied their orders

215

and took part; but the sense of a dance was over, and the cries that split the air told the difference.

"Sweet Maker," breathed Paragrin, "it's a massacre." Her arm was grabbed, and she spun about to attack, but the hold was Jentessa's.

"Come with me," said the woman.

"They're my people!" cried Paragrin, struggling in her grasp, which had grown unexpectedly strong.

"You won't help them by dying," said Jentessa, and she pulled her firmly from the fight, both of them emerging, miraculously unharmed, at the other side.

"But I shouldn't be here," said Paragrin, looking out on the battle. "I'm their leader."

"Jentessa's right to keep you out," said Cam. "You must survive, but I—I'll do what I can."

"Stay where you are," said the woman.

"But Jentessa, I have no reason to—"

"Don't argue!" she returned, in so angry a tone that Cam, much impressed, stayed where he was.

Suddenly Atanelle loomed out of the mass in front of them, brandishing a blade to defend herself from a red-bearded man. Paragrin saw at once that he was the one who had sat at Kerk's table in the Melde, and was frightened by him again as he forced her friend back with his spear. The warrior was strong, but he was clever, and when he had pushed her back almost to the wall, he faked a jab to her neck. She raised her knife to intercept, but he, victorious, turned his wrist and thrust his spear to her unprotected side. Atanelle's face twisted with pain, and as she fell, the man smiled and disappeared again in the crowd.

216

Cam caught his breath, and ran out to the warrior. He lifted her head to his lap, and tearing his jacket, used the cloth to stay the blood. Atanelle was pale, and looked up at him feebly.

"Ah, Cam . . . what a lovely surprise," she murmured.

"Don't talk," he said, and dabbed more gently at the wound. He looked away so she couldn't see the tears in his eyes.

Paragrin stared at her friend lying helpless on the ground, and the horror within her turned to rage. *She* was not helpless. If the earth had gone mad, if everyone was going to kill each other, she would not stand by and watch. The Glorious Ruler of the Ductae would leave her mark on them all.

She broke from the safety of the wall, and ran to the warrior, ignoring Jentessa's cry to return. "I'll get him, Atanelle, I swear it!" she said.

"Paragrin! What are you doing?" Cam exclaimed.

But she was determined; the passion of vengeance was upon her. She glared back at him through another's eyes and, seizing the warrior's knife, disappeared through the crowd.

"Dear Maker," Cam shuddered, "she looks like Zessiper."

Into the tangle of bodies she went, searching for the beard, the man who had struck down her friend. Wolf tails were everywhere, but she saved her first blow for him. There! At the other side of the square, his face stretched again into a smile as he raised his spear. Paragrin moved, and came upon him from behind. Her face

217

glowed with the glory of the coming kill, and she leaped forward, feet first, and knocked the spear from his hand. The red beard spun around, enraged, but before he could draw his blade, she threw herself against him. His eyes bulged as her knife sank into his flesh, and he opened his mouth to speak. No words came; he fell. Paragrin stood over him, the battle raging on around her, still grasping the blade in her hand. She was glad; she was glad for what she had done; and yet, as the man floundered on the ground, his mouth opening and closing in uneven, tortured gasps, pity rose up and overtook her. She dropped the knife, and falling to her knees, reached out to him with her hand; but the man, in his last breath, finally worked his blade free from its sheath, and struck out at her. She gasped as the weapon cut into her skin, and the man dropped the blade, and was still.

She staggered up and stumbled from the crowd, clutching at her arm. The wound wasn't lethal, but as the blood dripped down her fingers, she knew it was only time before another blade would claim her. She leaned up against the wall, appalled that she could be so capable of murder. And yet the violence was everywhere, it was infectious, out of control. Any sense of a purpose, of a cause, was gone, and the only incentive of all the killing was to stay alive. As Paragrin gazed sadly into the square, she saw only fear in the faces, confusion . . . as if they were all prisoners of the blades they swung.

All at once a boy broke from the crowd, and threw himself at the wall beside her, desperately trying to scramble over it, to escape, but just as he reached the

218

top a spear shot through the air and struck him, toppling him back to the ground. The spearman and the boy were both from Trag's army. They had begun, even, to turn against themselves.

On the other side of the chaos, Cam, still bracing Atanelle in his arms, looked in vain to the crowd to see Paragrin coming back to him; but he knew the tide of the battle, as well. Three bodies, one even of his fellow townsman, Nob, now lay motionless around him. Paragrin, he realized, might never come back.

"Jentessa!" he cried, his voice faint over the screams of the wounded. "Jentessa, she's gone. *Do* something!"

He looked to her, but she wasn't listening—to him, or to anything else he could see. She stood still beside the terror of the battle, alone, at peace; even her eyes were closed.

"Won't you even look at what's happening?" Cam sobbed. "Jentessa, open your eyes and see what's become of us. . . ."

And then, without any warning, he lurched forward, his body shaking uncontrollably.

"I've been hit," he thought, but as he raised his head to know his attacker, he saw with astonishment that everyone—the villagers and the fighters in the square—had fallen to the ground, sprawled out among the victims. The attacker had not been a person, but the earth itself; and it trembled now, ominously.

"Dear Essai," he breathed, and looked in wonder back to Jentessa. She alone stood firm and, with her eyes now opened, watched silently the confusion in the square.

Paragrin stared at the ground, amazed, her arms thrust

above her head to fend off the shower of debris that came tumbling down from the wall.

Trag, his eyes wide, pulled himself up to stand on the earth. "What's the matter?" he cried. "What's stopped the fighting?"

The people, still flat on the ground, stared back at him.

"What are you afraid of?" Trag demanded. "You're cowards, all of you!"

"The Center speaks," came a voice, and Trag, turning, saw the terrible eyes holding him again. "The fighting," Jentessa concluded, "the killing, must stop."

"No!" shouted Trag. "Who *are* you? Why have you come here?" He backed away to the wall near Paragrin, his eyes never leaving Jentessa. "Why have you come?"

"Your time is over," she said. "The land must return to the way it was. The Maker wills it so."

"Who are you to speak for the Maker?" Trag demanded.

The earth gave another threatening lurch, and the people, who had risen slightly to watch the confrontation, went down again.

A second shower of wood came from the barrier, and Trag, with his face gone white, fell back, staring with even greater horror at Jentessa.

"Father," called Paragrin, getting to her feet a little apart from where he stood, "listen to her! She knows what she's saying. Please, let it stop!" and the people, grateful, looked to Trag to accept the end. But he only turned on Paragrin.

"You!" he hissed. His eyes were strange, possessed,

220

and Paragrin backed away, alarmed. "You said that I rejected the Maker. You've brought all this down upon me, haven't you?"

She stared at him. He swayed unsteadily, and stepped toward her.

"You and your mother. She was hateful! She kept the Amulet hidden. She hid it all those years so that you could come in the end and finish her work, turning my men against me, turning the *Maker* against me! But I won't let her do it. I won't!"

He lunged forward and caught Paragrin by the throat. She struck out wildly, afraid at first for her life; but then as his massive hands moved from her neck to the chain she wore, she knew.

"No!" she cried, but was helpless to stop him. He wrenched the Amulet free from its chain, and flung her, defeated, to the ground.

Crazed with the glory of his prize, Trag scrambled to the top of the wall, and held it high above him. "The Oval Amulet!" he exulted. "I have it at last. I've *won*!" But then a strange, galloping sound rose up behind him. He turned, surprised, the Amulet still clasped in his hand. "Oh, my Maker . . ." he breathed, and Zessiper leaped to the top of the wall and upon him before he could even scream, thrusting her spear to his heart. He toppled from his height like a great stone falling, and Zessiper, with a joyous cry, rode his corpse to the ground.

The people gasped, unbelieving; and Paragrin, too astonished to speak, watched as Zessiper quietly took the Oval from Trag's lifeless grasp, and cradled it gently

221

in her hands. The old leader raised her head then and looked out at the faces, confused.

"Grandmother!" came the voice at last.

Zessiper turned, and when she saw Paragrin coming toward her, her eyes lit up with a glorious light. The old Ruler held the Oval out to the new, and Paragrin took it, going to her embrace.

"The Enemy is gone," whispered Zessiper, trembling in her arms. "It is all of it over!"

"Yes, my Own," said Paragrin, smiling through her tears, "it's over."

37

At evening, when the stars emerged lazily from behind the blue again—as if this day had been no different from any other—a heavy stillness lay across the ravaged land of Lexterre. The dead, totaling over a hundred, were buried now among the trees in the forest, and the remaining people of the diverse populations sat pensive around the fires in the square. The weeping and the celebration had ended, and the only sound that rose above the hush was music, sweet and sad, that came from the wooden flute.

Cam played, the pipe tucked between his lips, to Atanelle, who lay with the other wounded mending by the fires. When he finished, the warrior clapped her hands.

"Ah, I knew you'd be able to make that flute sing

when I gave it to you!" she exclaimed.

"You gave him the flute?" asked Paragrin, who had come herself, to listen.

"She not only gave it, she *made* it," said Cam.

"Well, there was extra wood in the cave," replied the warrior. "You understand."

"Oh, I understand," said Paragrin, and smiling, left them to continue the concert in peace.

Along the square the remnants of the wall still stood, a foot of barrier here, two feet there, nothing but rubble in other places. The scars of battle surrounded her, yet the Ruler, as she looked out on her people, took comfort. Men and women sat beside each other now, Ductae and Colonists, townspeople and fighters, for the sense of their separateness had already begun to fade with the common joys and sorrows that they felt. Despite everything, Paragrin knew this reunion had made the bloody battle worthwhile.

And then her complacent gaze fell on Aridda. The widow sat by herself at the farthest fire, and as Paragrin stiffened, the woman looked up slowly to meet her eyes, the light from the flames quivering against her face.

"Paragrin!"

She turned, relieved, to see Ellagette.

"Someone said we weren't going to stay in Lexterre anymore," remarked the girl. "Is it really true?"

"For now, at least," said Paragrin, amused by the eagerness in her voice. "It's important to have everyone united in the Melde . . . and I'm sure Kerk will be glad to see you, too," she added.

"I wasn't thinking about Kerk," Ellagette retorted,

reddening. "I'm just tired of this place, that's all. Actually, I've decided to have nothing more to do with men; I'm going to become like one of those warriors of yours and be independent."

Paragrin raised an eyebrow.

"I mean it," insisted the girl, and defiantly pulled off the cap that still confined her hair. Her long auburn tresses tumbled to her waist, and Paragrin, pulling impatiently at her own hair, sighed. "I'm going to wear it twisted, as they do," continued Ellagette. "You'll show me how, won't you, before we leave for the Colony?"

"Of course," said Paragrin, "but it looks very pretty the way it is."

"I know," returned the girl, "but as I said, I'm going to have nothing more to do with men"—and she moved away, tossing her head disdainfully as Cam walked past her.

"Is something wrong with Ellagette?" he asked.

"I don't know," said Paragrin, staring after her. "Kerk may be in for a surprise."

"Well!" came a voice, and the companions turned to see Jentessa before them. "I've heard of some lovely news about the camp tonight," said the Intermediator, clasping their hands. "The two of you are going to be Joined."

"Yes! I was going to tell you earlier," said Paragrin, "but things were a little . . . confusing."

"To say the least," returned Jentessa. "Well, I am truly surprised and delighted."

"You don't look surprised," Cam observed.

"Jentessa," said the Ruler, after a moment had passed,

225

"I've been meaning to ask you about . . . well, about why you were so late in coming this morning."

"Was I late?"

"If you had come only a little earlier . . ."

". . . Yes?"

"Well, maybe Strap wouldn't have been killed."

"In every age there are victims," the woman returned. "That is the Maker's will."

Paragrin studied her in silence, then looked away. "That man beside me in the mural, it never was Strap, was it?" She turned back and confronted her. "Who is going to be the male ruler, Jentessa?"

"I do not decide," said the woman. "As Holy Intermediator, I only help the Maker choose. Tell me," she said, turning to Cam, "I respect your opinion; what sort of person would *you* choose to rule beside our headstrong friend?"

He looked to Paragrin and smiled. "Just to even things out, perhaps one a little less impulsive."

"Yes! And what else?"

Cam grew thoughtful. "Well, ideally he should have a different view of leadership, shouldn't he?—one that was compatible with hers, but different enough so that all types of people might be served. That's what the double rule is supposed to be about, isn't it? A woman and a man striking a balance between them, one that's stronger than anything they would have by themselves?"

"Exactly so," said Jentessa. "I see you remember what was taught you in the cave. . . . I thought you would."

Paragrin looked at Jentessa, then at Cam, then back again to Jentessa, her eyes widening.

226

"Well, it's fine to stand here and idealize," said the young man, "but the fact is, there's no one of the Ruling Family left. I don't know who you're going to find."

Jentessa drew the Rectangular iron from her cloak and placed it in his hand. "I've found him," she said.

Cam stared at the Amulet, confused. "Oh, my Maker!" he cried, suddenly realizing her intent. "Jentessa, *I* can't be Ruler!" and he thrust the iron back at her.

"Why not?"

"Sweet Divine! I'm not the ruler *type*. I'm not at all like Paragrin."

"You are, perhaps, a little less impulsive," said the woman, "and you *do* have a somewhat different view of leadership, but it's compatible with hers. It seems to me that together, you might strike a balance, and the greatest number of people could be served. That is what the double rule is supposed to be about . . . isn't it?"

Cam stared at her, open-mouthed. "Then that's why you wouldn't let me fight in the battle," he said at last. "You were afraid I might be—"

"It is not in your nature to fight," said Jentessa. "If I had let you go, you would have been among the first to die."

"He's as strong as any of the soldiers," said Paragrin. "He could have stood up to them as well as anyone else."

"But . . . I'm not sure I could have killed them," said Cam slowly, and he glanced at her. "It's not that I think it's wrong to do it in defense, it's just . . . so repugnant to me." He forced a laugh. "It's a good thing

227

Kerk can't hear. He'd call it cowardice; perhaps he's right."

Paragrin shook her head. "No one who would offer his life for the Oval could be a coward."

"His is an uncommon creed," said Jentessa, "but a dangerous one. It will be up to you, Paragrin, to watch out for him." She closed his fingers gently over the iron. "You should know I would never betray the Maker's trust by suggesting a man incapable of doing the Rectangle justice. You can do it more than justice, Cam; you can do it honor."

He looked down at the iron, his face tight with apprehension.

"Cam," said Paragrin, and she laid her hand on his arm, "you said I was chosen, well, so have you been, now. And if you back down after all we've been through . . . I swear I'll never forgive you."

He looked up at her, uncertain, but the doubt in his eyes softened. "All right," he said at last, "we'll do it, then. Together."

"Splendid!" said Jentessa. "And we'll have the ceremony of the Passing here, tonight, for all these weary people to see. Come, my young leader," she exclaimed, taking his hand, "we have many things to discuss." And she gave Paragrin a delighted smile, as she led him away.

Paragrin smiled herself, she was so amazed and relieved by the whole resolution. To think that if things had gone differently she might have been forced to have . . . Strap; and she was suddenly ashamed of her own relief. Over by the farthest fire the widow still sat alone, and after a moment of awful debate, Paragrin found herself walking toward her. Too soon, she was there, and the hollow eyes rose up again, slowly, to repulse her.

"Get away from me," she hissed.

"Aridda, I'm *sorry*."

"Oh, yes," said the woman. "Things have gone quite badly for you, haven't they? It's all these people can talk about, how fine and brave their new young leader is. Well, we know it better, don't we, Paragrin?"

"I only did what I had to do," said the Ruler. "In the end, I think even Strap understood that." She paused. "I—I wish you could have been there, Aridda," she said quietly, "to see how he touched my hand before he died. For a second, we knew each other." Paragrin looked away, not wanting the woman to see her face. "I haven't forgotten my duty to you. There'll be room at the Rulers' House at the Melde; if, someday, you come to realize that the Maker lives there as much as here, you're welcome to stay." And without meeting her gaze, she left.

And Aridda, the glow from the flames trembling against her, turned back to the fire, silent.

When Jentessa had versed Cam in his role for the ceremony, she gathered the people together and told them how their sacrifice that day would be honored by the chance to witness their new Ruler's accession to power. Whether it was the anticipation of the rare event or the brightness of the woman's eyes that had roused them, they came, some held up by others, to take part—for the second time that day—in history.

229

Jentessa went to show Paragrin her place, and as she led her forward she slipped an arm about her shoulders. "It must not have been easy to talk to Aridda," Jentessa said softly. "It's upset you."

"A little," the Ruler admitted. "I don't know, I never used to care how she felt. I just wish she wouldn't *blame* me so."

"Give her time. She's suffered much today."

Paragrin nodded. "And just think what this ceremony will do to her on top of everything else, to see another man get the Rectangle. Oh!" she breathed, suddenly taking Jentessa's arm. "What about Zessiper? She's not going to see this, is she?"

"Your grandmother is asleep in a house," said the woman. "Her afflictions are such that she shouldn't wake until morning. Don't worry. Now stand here in front, Paragrin, the time has come to begin," and she drew from her cloak a familiar little box, filled with sandy earth.

And then Jentessa looked out upon the people, and a hush fell across them. They watched in silence, expectantly, as the woman slowly closed her eyes and began, the soft resonance of the chant rising from her lips.

"Laudais lu chemnee garai,"

she recited.

"Essai, fee dem tran cetus."

The words were strange to most, but filled them all with a sense of wonder, as if somehow the Maker Itself were suddenly among them.

230

Cam, his moment come at last, walked slowly toward Jentessa, his eyes held straight in front of him. When he reached her, he knelt, and she sprinkled the dirt over him, saying,

"The Earth envelops and stays the body,
But the spirit, everlasting, returns;
Back to the Center, back to the Maker,
Back to Essai, united, forever."

Paragrin smiled to hear the measures again, as if they reaffirmed her own sacred rulership as much as Cam's— a comfort after Aridda's disapproval. Yet to another, alone in the darkness, the old strain struck a different chord. She sat up, her eyes suddenly wide and staring, listening for the narrative she had heard in her dreams. "In the beginning, there was Essai, the Maker, at the Center. . . ." The words of the Passing were there; they were real! She cocked her head, confused, and, tossing aside her blanket, padded across the floor, and out into the night.

With her eyes half closed, Paragrin allowed Jentessa's words to blend softly in her mind. Everything seemed extraordinary then, the brilliance of the stars, the sweetness in the air, the new dignity of her companion as he stood now straight and tall before Jentessa. Who would have thought such a perfect end could be had from this tragic day? She had never felt so thrilled nor so peaceful in her life.

"Within these irons are the blessings of the Maker," said Jentessa, "and they have been passed down for generation upon generation, to secure, with each succession, the promise of earthly prosperity.

"As it was for the first Colonists, so it is today. The passing and the promise continue."

The walker in the night, more troubled then ever by the unexpected gathering, moved steadily forward through the crowd, determined to see the cause, putting the people from her path.

"And as it was for Trag, as it was for Ram," said the Holy Intermediator, her arms lifted out to her sides, "as it was for the race of male rulers back to Veer the Half-Divine, so it is for you." She placed the Amulet over Cam's bowed head. "Hail, Cam. Hail, the new Ruler of the Melde!"

Paragrin drew back from her reverie to see Cam turning to the people. He seemed so pleased, she couldn't help but smile, the Rectangle looked so majestic against his chest. Then her heart stopped; for there, looking with horror out at the scene, was Zessiper.

"No!" she cried.

Cam turned, surprised, and the next moment, he was hurled to the ground, Zessiper crouching on top of him, her eyes wild again, her lean brown fingers clenched about his throat.

The crowd screamed. Paragrin stared at the struggle, too appalled, at first, to move; then she broke from her ground and fell upon Zessiper, trying to pull her free from Cam. With a strength known only to desperation, she succeeded; Zessiper, her hands clawing the air, was tight in her grip, and Paragrin twisted her about to face her. Immediately, the old Ruler's face went slack; she looked back at Paragrin with an awful amazement.

"Tempira," she breathed, "you're alive!"

232

Paragrin's grip on her loosened; she looked back at her, stunned.

"I thought he had murdered you," said Zessiper softly, reaching out to stroke her face. "I was going to kill him, again."

Paragrin glanced at Jentessa, who, having helped Cam to his feet, stared at her now, her eyes turned grim and steady.

"I—I'm here, Mother," said Paragrin, forcing herself to look back at her. "There's no need to hurt anyone. It's over . . . remember?"

"I thought it was over," Zessiper murmured. "I was just so confused. . . ."

Jentessa moved forward and, with a nod to Paragrin, turned the old Ruler toward herself. Zessiper went willingly. "Is it time, Jentessa?" she asked faintly.

"Yes, I think it's time," said the woman, and with a quick, light movement, she caught the old Ruler up in her arms. Zessiper lay still, her head pressed against the woman's cloak. "Are you all right?" Jentessa asked, turning to Cam.

"Yes, I think so," he answered, coming to stand beside Paragrin. "Is . . . she?"—and he stared, wondering at the ease with which Jentessa held her.

The woman shook her head. "No," she replied, "but she will be, soon enough. The ceremony has ended," she announced suddenly to the people. "I suggest everyone leave now and take to a bed." She gave the crowd a look that made even the most curious back away, and soon only the companions remained in the square.

She gazed at them, and gave a sad smile. "I did so

233

want to go with you to the Colony," she said, "just to help you get started, and witness your Joining in person."

"Where are you going?" asked Paragrin, her eyes still fixed on the docile figure of her grandmother in the woman's arms.

"Home," said Jentessa. "I have always known that my work would be finished when Zessiper's time had ended, and so it is. I just misjudged when it would come. I forget, sometimes, how very delicate you people are."

Paragrin moved her gaze slowly to Jentessa. "What do you mean by that?" she said.

"What about Zessiper?" asked Cam. "How should we care for her?"

"Don't worry about Zessiper," said the woman. "I've cared for her for almost forty years, and I'll care for her now. You two concentrate of the life ahead of you; that's where your duty lies. It won't be easy, but I have no doubt you'll succeed. I am not afraid to leave the Melde in your care."

"I don't understand," said Paragrin. "What do you mean by 'leave'?"

"Good-bye," said Jentessa, and backed away.

"Good-bye?" Paragrin echoed.

Jentessa closed her eyes, and Cam saw the same peaceful seclusion spread over her face that she had worn before the earthquake. He took Paragrin's hand and held it, prepared for anything.

"Essai," called Jentessa, in a voice so soft that the companions had to strain their ears to hear it. "Essai, it is I, Jentessa, your seventh-born."

Paragrin's eyes widened.

"It is done. The Unity You envisioned and kept here for so long has been restored. I leave the Melde more fully now, to Your Rulers' care."

Cam's hand tightened around Paragrin's.

"But if there should ever be a day when they have need of me," whispered Jentessa, opening her eyes and gazing out at them one more time, "I pray that You will allow me to come again. It is not easy to leave these people, though You may think that strange. I have grown to love, among these mortals, and I love *them*, very much." Her eyes almost seemed to fill with tears, then, and Paragrin, her own eyes brimming, reached out to catch at her with her hand. But though she touched her, there was nothing more to feel. Jentessa and the broken figure in her arms were fading into the darkness around them, fading, until there was nothing left to see but the trees.

Paragrin sank to the ground and wept; but the tears were good tears, and Cam held her until the darkness itself faded and gave way to morning.

38

When all the wounded were well enough to travel, the company of survivors left Lexterre and began the journey back to the Melde. The days were fair and full with spring, and there was time in the cool evenings to sit by the River and dream about the future.

One person did more than dream; the young soldier Mott, who had been pressed into the army against his wishes, ran home ahead of the others to tell his family and all the long-suffering citizens of the Melde that they were finally free. And when at last Paragrin and Cam led the long parade of villagers, Ductae, and soldiers into the central court, the Colonists welcomed the new beginning with a festival such as the Good Earth had never seen before.

Kerk was there, cheering louder than anyone else.

He laughed when he saw his brother with the Rectangle, for he thought Cam looked stuffy, and told him so, but he clapped him on the back anyway and gave Little Gret a warm embrace. Yet when he saw Ellagette among the survivors, an eagerness welled up in him that the sisters of the cave and Colony had never quite been able to match. Did Ellagette notice his renewed admiration? She did; and be it known that within the hour the piece of twine that had bound her defiant braid was found discarded in a field.

After the celebration Paragrin and Cam made their way to the Rulers' house at the head of the court and, after carefully removing Trag's bearskin that had served as a door, went in to see how they would live. They explored the ancient stone hallways and chambers in quiet reverence, until they finally moved aside the door of the last room and jumped to see someone already there.

"You gave me a fright," said Aridda, who had nearly dropped the bundle of clothes in her arms. "Next time I'll expect you to announce yourselves." She glared at them, and put the clothes into a chest that stood against the wall.

Cam and Paragrin exchanged a glance.

"As you can see, I've decided to stay," said Aridda, "though it won't be on charity. I'll be the Keeper of the House while I'm here. I'll make the chambers clean and do the cooking. *All* the cooking," she added, frowning at Cam. "And when you have children, I'll watch for them, too. I'm sure you'll be much too concerned with your work, Paragrin, to take proper care."

"I—I don't know what to say," faltered the Ruler.

"Enough's been said. Now go along and do what you have to do. There's too much on my hands to stand here and chat"—and she turned away to straighten the chest. The companions exchanged another look and went out from the room.

"Well, this should make you happy," said Cam.

"I'm delighted," Paragrin returned.

"Ah, my Glorious Rulers!" said a voice, and Atanelle came marching down the passageway pulling a small middle-aged man with thinning hair behind her. "I've found someone to perform your Joining," said the warrior, holding the little man out. "This is Notts. He's nothing compared to Jentessa, but it's said he knows religion well enough. Down on your knees, Notts, these are your new leaders."

The man, who had been staring at the two companions with something between awe and rapture, fell to the ground—with some assistance from Atanelle—and hung his head.

"It's all right," said Cam, helping the man up again. "So you know how to do Joinings, do you? Were you the Holy Intermediator when Trag was here?"

"Oh my, no," said the man. "There was never a proper Holy person then, but my father knew a lot about it all from when religion was more generally known, back before Ram and all. I—I'd be very honored to do your service this afternoon, if you'll have me," and he stared up at them again, full of wonder. "I just think this is the most marvelous thing to happen since . . . since I don't know when. You both look so fine and knowledgeable."

238

"Tell me," said Paragrin, slowly stepping forward, "what gender do you use when you speak of Essai in the Joining ceremony?"

"Oh, no gender at all, of course," said the man. "I never did believe your father's lies."

Paragrin smiled. "I like him," she said to Cam, then turned back to Notts. "Could you be ready in an hour, out by the riverside?"

"Oh, absolutely!" His face shone with pleasure. "I'll go right now, and prepare." And bowing once again to the Rulers—as well as to Atanelle—he scurried out.

"You were lucky to find him," said Paragrin.

"Yes," said Atanelle, and her eyes widened. "Do you know I've never seen so many men in my life? That court is *full* of them! Why, it's practically more than I can take at one time."

Paragrin nodded. "And incidentally," she said, smiling, "I like what you did to your hair."

The warrior lowered her eyes. "Thank you," she murmured, stroking the brightly-colored ribbon that held her braid. "I suppose *you* might think a ribbon was silly," she said, glancing at Cam.

"Not at all," he replied. "It looks beautiful"—and the warrior turned a very deep shade of pink.

Suddenly a loud commotion was heard at the entrance to the house, and Atanelle, forgetting her braid in the instant, hurried out to see what it was. Within seconds she returned with a soldier and a warrior, who were dragging between them a wizened old man.

Cam and Paragrin went forward, and when the old man looked up, he stopped his swearing, and scowled.

Paragrin stepped back, her eyes flashing as she recognized him. "Ram!" she spat, and her hand curled around the blade at her belt. "The soldiers said you had gone with Trag to Lexterre. I thought you had died there."

"Too bad I didn't," Ram returned, his eyes narrowing as he gained his courage. "I followed you all back, though you didn't know it, and I would have kept apart from you here if this traitor," he snarled, glaring at the soldier, "hadn't tripped over me in the grain storage. What do you hold me for? Stealing? A man has to eat."

"Not for long," said Paragrin, drawing her blade.

Ram cried out in anger and pushed back against his captors.

"Now, Paragrin," said Cam, staying her arm, "he's not worth killing. He's an old man."

"He's the one who started it all," she returned. "He's the one who started the lies, and drove my grandmother from the city!"

"I didn't drive her out," Ram returned. "She went of her own stupidity."

Paragrin raised the knife again, and Cam had to pull her back to stop her.

"That's right! Just kill me and be done with it," said Ram. "Approach everything with a knife, just as Zessiper did. Ah, it's a pity you aren't more like your *grandfather*. . . ."

"Paragrin, stop the violence," said Cam, trying to turn her from the old man's grin. "We're making a new life here. We're about to be Joined! Let's not start it off with blood on our hands."

Paragrin glowered at Ram, but lowered the blade to her side. "He's dangerous," she said.

240

"He's an old man. Let the Maker deal with him. He hasn't much longer to live, anyway," Cam added in a whisper.

She hesitated, but finally replaced the knife in its sheath. "All right, but I'm going to keep a watch on him. A *close* watch."

"He's got more sense than you," said Ram, nodding to Cam. "But then, any man would."

"Get him out of here," said Cam to the captors. "We have more important things to think about." And with Atanelle giving him an especially nasty tug, they pulled Ram out again into the court.

"He makes my blood burn," muttered Paragrin. "No wonder Zessiper couldn't stand to rule beside him."

"Forget him," said Cam, and he took her hands in his. "We have to get ready. Do you have the clothes for the ceremony?"

"Yes," said Paragrin. "They're in the main chamber, beside the bed."

"*Our* bed," smiled Cam, and slipped his arms around her waist.

Paragrin sighed. "Do you know, Partner," she said softly, "I think we're finally home."

And then the musicians, fifty strong, lined the path from the entrance to the grassy bank of the River Melde. As the afternoon sun burned brightly above them, they put their lips to the wood, their fingers to the strings, and their hands to the canvases, and in one initial blast that rolled across the water and bounded off the mountainsides, filled the air with music, and the hearts of

241

the Colonists—for they were all Colonists, now, even Atanelle—with the thrill and exhilaration of the regal Joining.

Notts, with his thinning hair combed back and his eyes nearly bursting with pleasure, presided over it all, and when the two companions, splendent in their flowers and brightly colored linens, came together before him, he held his arms out to enfold them.

"In the beginning," he proclaimed, "there was the One, the Maker, the Only; and in that Unity was a great Peace and Joy. Essai saw that it was good.

"And then It created the Two, the Woman and the Man, for It saw that this also was good, that from the Two could come many, to populate and care for Its earth.

"But the Maker was wise. It knew that the Peace could be threatened by this making, that there could always be a chance of a Separation between the Two, a Sorrow without the Unity, even," he said sadly, "the chance of a battle between them, for such is the nature, sometimes, of a division.

"So Essai in Its wisdom created another, stronger nature, and this It called Love and Caring—that nature that gives the Two the glory of the One again. And that is why this ceremony of Love between the Two is sacred, and is called the Joining."

Notts lowered his hands and took up a large wooden cup filled with water from the River. "Drink from the Unity," he said, holding forth the cup, and Cam and Paragrin, hands clasped, drank together.

He grinned. "The blessing of the Maker is upon you. May your One be ever eternal."

242

The companions looked from him to one another, incredulous, and Joined again in a kiss. The crowd burst into cheers, and some of the people cried to see the old promise come to life again before them, while the musicians, forgetting all decorum, blasted their music to the world.